LOVE AND PROZAC

Gary G. Gilberg

GARY G. GILBERG

Published by Gary G. Gilberg.

Paperback edition ISBN:978-0-9987468-1-4
Hardback edition ISBN:978-0-9987468-2-1

Book layout by ebooklaunch.com

FROM THE AUTHOR

This book is written as a literary novel, though it has elements of a memoir, threads of counseling and scenes evocative of a movie script. At its core, it's a love story, but a mature rendition, full of human frailty, compassion and forgiveness.

If you have ever experienced a serious bout of depression, there may be scenes in the book that trigger unresolved feelings. If you choose to put down the book, I understand completely. My intent is not to harm, but to engage and enlighten. Rest assured this is a story of struggle and triumph, not capitulation.

Fifty percent of all Americans will suffer a bout of some form of mental illness during their lifetime, whether it be depression, anxiety, bulimia or other psychiatric disorders. These conditions are not character defects. They are medical in nature. I wrote Love and Prozac to help break the silence that stigmatizes half of the American population.

Part One

"Little Alice fell down the hole,
bumped her head and bruised her soul."[1]

(Lewis Carroll, Alice in Wonderland)

CHAPTER 1

I drift out of a dense fog, clenching the sides of the mattress with my sweaty palms. A flickering light above my head casts shadows against the wall like an old movie projector. On the screen Dad bounces me up and down on his knee while my brother Daniel mugs for the camera in the background. Waves crash against the wooden pilings below the Santa Monica pier. The water rolls up the sand and my brother dissolves into the white foam.

A whiff of ammonia jolts me back into my concrete cell. The walls move, closing in around me. I stand up and hobble towards the metal door across the room. The room spins like a top, ready to topple. I lunge for the door handle as my legs liquefy. Just before my head hits, I think, "This is going to hurt."

"We have a patient who fell in room twelve. I need a nurse right away. Are you OK?"

I try to reply, but the words shrivel on my tongue. My body is lifted onto the bed, but I'm strangely detached, as if watching a play from the upper balcony seats. Looking down on the stage, I see a hole above my left eye. My brains spill onto the sheets. Grey matter oozes everywhere. I grab a clump of cortex and stuff it back into my skull. I search frantically, but I can't find the missing shard of bone. For God's sake, plug the hole!

I'm losing control.

"Line up for your morning meds."

I'm curled in a fetal position. My head throbs, a piñata about to burst open. I lift my hand and trace the edges of my eye socket. It's swollen shut.

Where's Christy?

I slowly ease my head off the bed. Light streams through louvred shades, weaving prison stripes across my shirt. An empty mattress rests across the room, a stack of white sheets folded neatly at one end. Two small dressers sit opposite corners, their pulls drooping at odd angles. Beside each dresser is a wardrobe closet and matching chair, a spider web of sorrow strung across the seats. I lay my head back down.

I need to get those drawings started for the Andersons. I haven't worked in over a year.

"Erik. Mr. Scott. Wake up." My head is buried in the fog. I strain to open my eyes.

"I'm here to look at that gash on your head." Deep green eyes floating over blue hospital scrubs stare back at me.

"I'm Nurse Lisa. How are you feeling this morning?"

"Where am I?"

"You're in the Combine County Behavioral Health Clinic."

"How did I get here?"

"You were brought here last night from Barton Hospital on a 5150."

"What's that?"

"It's a seventy-two hour hold for patients considered a danger to themselves or others."

This is a mistake.

"Where's my wife?"

"Maybe Dr. Williams can answer that. He's making his morning rounds." She puts her hand on my shoulder, "Can I take a look at that cut over your eye?"

"OK."

"You had us worried last night."

Her soft fingers delicately lift the skin across my forehead. With clinical precision, she cleans the gash over my eyebrow with a sterile wipe and clears the dried blood.

"You won't need any stitches, but you'll have a black eye for a few days."

I nod.

"Dr. Williams will stop by in a few minutes." She strides out the door.

Gazing down at my feet, I see powder blue socks sprinkled with white rubber dots. The dots form a happy face that stares back at me and then blinks.

Did I just I hallucinate?

I look again… just random dots.

CHAPTER 2

Slender green tentacles wrap themselves around my frontal lobe. My head jerks back and I gag, my mouth flooding with a torrent of water.

I must be dreaming.

"Hello, Mr. Scott, are you up?"

"I'm in the shower."

"Take your time. I'll come back in ten minutes."

I towel off and hobble into the bedroom. My left knee and back throb like the time I got bucked off the mechanical bull at a cowboy bar trying to impress Christy. I slowly slip on faded blue jeans, a t-shirt and my favorite dimpled socks, then sit down on the empty mattress across from my bed. I reach into my back pocket for my phone to call her. It's not there. I check all my pockets. No phone or wallet. I look up to see a man wearing beige cargo shorts and a white lab coat with "Dr. Williams," on his lapel.

"Hello, Mr. Scott, can I call you Erik?"

Under the lab coat a bright orange and blue Hawaiian shirt is visible, splashing hibiscus flowers across his chest. His sun-tanned legs are stocky and covered in blond peach fuzz. He's wearing brown leather penny loafers with no socks. Minus the lab coat, he could have just stepped off his sailboat after winning the Tahoe yacht club regatta. I try to lift myself off the bed. He reaches over and helps me into a sitting position.

"Sure, call me Erik."

"How are you feeling this morning?"

The orange hibiscus flowers are reassuring.

"Where's my phone and wallet?"

"We don't allow cell phones or valuables in the clinic."

"Where's Christy?"

"I have no information about your wife."

"I don't remember how I got here."

"You have amnesia."

"From what?"

"You tried to commit suicide."

"I'd never do that." This is all a bad dream.

"Apparently you did."

"Why can't I remember?"

"It could be the result of a concussion, severe emotional trauma or a combination."

"I don't belong here."

"No one does," he says, looking me in the eye. "My job is to get you quickly stabilized and back on your feet."

"You won't keep me locked up."

"Our average patient stay is one month."

"How did I get this?" I ask, touching the gash on my forehead.

"You came in last night heavily sedated. Apparently, you got out of bed and fell. I'll put you on Seroquel tonight. It's easier to tolerate. Is that OK?"

They put Daniel in a catatonic stupor.

"My brother committed suicide on antipsychotic drugs. I don't trust them."

"Have you ever tried to commit suicide before?"

"Of course not."

"Then let's see it doesn't happen again."

I stroke my chin and discover three-day old stubble. Christy said it scratched the first time we kissed. I've been clean shaven ever since.

"I don't know."

"Medication, combined with therapy, is your best chance at a full recovery."

I take a few seconds to collect my thoughts.

"What if I say no to the drugs?"

"We can't force you, but you already were given anti-psychotic drugs when you tried to commit suicide. You were sedated for two days to protect yourself."

Maybe that's why I'm so loopy.

"They did that without my permission?"

"You were deemed incapable of making a rational decision."

If I agree to take them, I'll gain some control of the situation. I just need to hold myself together long enough to get out of here.

"You're in a psychiatric emergency," he says. "If you had a life-threatening bacterial infection in your brain right now, would you take a pill to fight the infection?"

"Sure."

"This is no different. You have a chemical imbalance in your brain.

"Will it knock me silly like last night?"

"I'll adjust the dose. Be sure to move slowly when you get out of bed."

"OK, let's switch to the Sorrowkill."

He spells it out, "S-E-R-O-Q-U-E-L."

I close my eyes and repeat the letters in my head for a few seconds. The word dissolves. It terrified me to realize my mind was failing. The once powerful instrument of reason that conquered calculus, breezed through the California

Architectural exam and courted Christy with reckless abandon suddenly turned on me; from inquisitive and analytical, perceptive and confident, my mind wouldn't focus, constantly belittled me.

"I can write that down for you," the doctor says.

I nod. He pulls a small leather-bound notepad and black ballpoint pen from his hip pocket. Opening up the cover, he scribbles on the top page, tears it out and hands it to me. I look down. Sister Mary Ellen, my first-grade English teacher, would have slapped her ruler across his knuckles. It's completely illegible. I set it on the wardrobe to my right.

"Do you have any questions?" he asks.

"I've never been in a place like this."

"Each day is broken into sixteen hour long segments, each hour planned out on the schedule. You start with morning medication, then breakfast. I've got you starting with twenty milligrams of Prozac[2] this morning. Are you familiar with it?"

"I have a friend taking it." He calls it his happy pill.

"Prozac is an antidepressant. Technically it's an SSRI, or selective serotonin reuptake inhibitor. We've had good results with it."

I could use happy.

"After breakfast we have our Community meeting where you get together with the other patients and review your mood and goals for the day. Patients then break up into smaller groups for a variety of therapy sessions throughout the day."

An ant winds his way across the floor next to the doctor's penny loafer. He's lost. He'll get crushed if he isn't careful.

We have smoke breaks and an exercise period after lunch. There's quiet time after dinner then the Evening

Wrap Up meeting. More medication is dispensed at 9 p.m. and it's lights out at 10 p.m. I make my rounds in the morning. That's when I'll check in with you."

The ant probes the shoe with his antennae. He scurries away.

Nurse what's her name pops her head in the door.

"Sorry to interrupt. The dispensary is closing in a few minutes. It's time for your morning meds, Mr. Scott."

"No problem. We'll be done in a minute," the doctor says.

The ant disappears into a crack in the baseboard. He's safe at home now.

"We're here to help, Erik," he says, "but you determine the outcome."

I rub my forehead. Someone's pounding the piñata again.

"I'm in, doc," I say. He smiles and turns to walk out. "I need to call Christy."

"I'll have Nurse Lisa get an outside line for you after breakfast."

I shuffle back to the bathroom. A fifty-seven-year old with a sunken chest and beer belly stands in the mirror. The bloated gash over his eye gives him the look of a washed-up actor in a mugshot after a drunken brawl.

"You're a mess," he says.

Billows of fog float up the glass, and he slowly disappears.

CHAPTER 3

As we enter the day room, I cover my eyes to shield them from the intense blue light. The hum of bees buzz in my ears. I see a nursing station in the center of a large room, a bank of computer terminals surrounded by a ring of counters. The brown cabinets form a blockade to protect the staff from unruly mobs. There's a red-headed woman in hospital scrubs playing her keyboard like a piano in front of a monitor, her hands dance across the keys. In the corner, I watch a tall black man with a shaved head pull down his pants to expose the soft flesh below his hip. Next to him a male nurse prepares a needle wearing blue gloves as a young blond gets her blood pressure checked by a grey-haired nurse. The girl rubs the sleep from her puffy eyes. A third nurse, much younger, is stationed behind a door to the right. The top half of the door is open and there's a stripe on the floor four feet away. A hand-written note is taped on the bottom half of the door. "Stand behind the line until your name is called." I toe my blue dimpled socks to the line.

"Erik, this is Nurse Ellen. She's in charge of medication."

"Good morning, Erik, please state your full name and date of birth."

I struggle to remember. "Erik Scott, born October 12, 1954."

"Erik, we have twenty milligrams of Prozac and five thousand international units of vitamin D-3 for you this morning. Would you like some Tylenol for that black eye?"

"Sure."

The nurse hands me a paper cup full of water and another full of pills. I gag trying to swallow and spit the pills back into the cup.

My hand shakes as the nurse gives me a second cup of water. "Swallow them one at a time," she says. I manage to swallow the vitamin D and Tylenol, but the Prozac recoils from my mouth and shoots onto the floor.

"Here, try two of these smaller Prozac tablets," she says. She gives me another cup. I manage to down them.

"Now open your mouth and stick out your tongue for Nurse Ellen to show you swallowed all your medicine," the head nurse says. Like a first grader at the school dispensary, I stick out my tongue.

Hold yourself together.

She leads me over to an empty chair next to the black man with the shaved head.

"Good morning, Charles," she says.

"Good morning," he bellows, grey whiskers poking from his sun crinkled chin.

"This is Erik, Charles. He was admitted late last night. Can you show him around this morning?"

"Of course, Nurse Lisa," he says, exposing a mouthful of yellow teeth and a receding gum line. Charles extends his calloused right hand in my direction while the male nurse plunges the syringe into his left hip. His handshake is firm, steady. I stare at the needle.

"You won't get shot in the ass. That's for my diabetes."

A thirty-something with disheveled brown hair stands up from one of the tables in the adjoining room. He yells across the room, "Charles, cover up your flabby bum! We're trying to eat breakfast over here."

I hear laughter. Charles smiles.

"That's Alex. He's one day into detox and starting withdrawals."

The nurse playing her keyboard in the station finishes her composition. I hear the birdlike squawk from a printer churning out pages.

"The first six days are the worst," Charles says. "Let's grab breakfast and I'll introduce you around."

CHAPTER 4

The dining hall looks like a homeless shelter at feeding time. An assortment of misfits grab food trays from a stainless-steel cart, stacked tall with the morning cuisine. The dress code is thrift store casual; droopy sweatpants, oversize t-shirts and couch slippers are popular. Some of the patients are already seated and stare down at their plates. Everyone moves at half speed. Charles searches through the food cart and emerges with two trays. He hands me one with my name on a white slip of paper. My name is misspelled. The tray overflows with pancakes, bacon, chocolate milk, orange juice, syrup, yogurt, butter and a fruit cup. I follow him over to a table with two empty chairs.

"It's the mayor, showing another newbie around," says Alex, the left side of his gaunt face quivers.

"Alex, this is Erik. He came in last night."

Alex sports a thin mustache and a gold earring in his left ear. He looks like a pirate with scurvy. Alex extends his hand and we share a tepid handshake.

I sit down and stare at my tray overflowing with food. Charles pours ketchup on his scrambled eggs and takes a big bite.

"Yikes!" he says, spitting gooey pink slime onto the table. "What's in this?"

"Hot sauce in the ketchup bottle," Alex says with a smirk, watching Charles gulp down the entire carton of juice on his tray. Alex slides his plateful of eggs in front of Charles.

"Here, you can have my eggs. No hard feelings?"

Charles wipes his mouth with a napkin.

"You owe me some smokes, Alex."

"Got one over on The Mayor," says Alex.

"The Mayor?" I say.

"Charles's an official in the clinic," the pirate says. "How many times have you been in here?"

"Relapse is part of recovery," Charles says.

"He's a meth ho," Alex says. I look over, expecting a fight to erupt.

"I can quit any time," Charles says with a glint in his pale green eyes.

"Community meeting in twenty minutes!" the head nurse calls out.

I get permission to call Christy after breakfast, but when I put the phone in my ear the line is dead. I try again, this time waiting for the dial tone before slowly tapping out her number with my right index finger. I get a recording.

"The number you have reached is no longer in service."

Nurse Lisa stares at me.

"Do you want some help?" My hand shakes as I hand her the phone.

"Please."

I give her the number. She dials and returns the phone. I hear Christy's voice.

"Hi honey, it's me," I say before realizing it's her voicemail. She finishes up.

"Please leave a message after the tone."

"I'm sorry. Are you OK? Please call."

I repeat the number from the clinic phone twice and then hang up.

• • •

I shuffle back to my room to brush my teeth. Leaning on the sink, I hold my head in my hands and grind my teeth. My chest constricts and beads of sweat drip from my armpits. I've lost my confidence. I was the Senior class president in high school. Christy, who had her pick of suitors, fell in love with me. What changed? A wave of nausea crashes over me. I crumble to my knees. My eyes close and I catch a glimpse of Christy with blood on her face. She shrinks and then disappears. I lurch into the dining area, gasping for breath.

Charles writes on a large whiteboard with a bright red pen. Several patients stand nearby, staring at the board. Charles turns and hands me a sheet of paper.

"Write down your mood and goals for the day," he says.

The paper, encased in clear plastic, illustrates forty emotions with facial expressions drawn in pen, from sad to happy and every variation in between. I gaze at the faces for a good three minutes. I grab a dark blue pen from the pile scattered haphazardly on the aluminum shelf under the whiteboard. I write "Erik" in the name column, "Depressed" as my mood, and "Make it through the day" as my goal for the day. I stand back and take in the whole board.

Sandy is despondent and her goal is to eat all the food on her lunch plate.

Alex is jumpy and his goal is to not have any flashbacks.

Troy is moody and his goal is to make himself laugh.

Gina is nervous and her goal is to keep up her guard.

Charles is reflective and his goal is to stay in the present.

A bearded man wearing a San Francisco Giants cap at the head of the room stumbles as he rises. He picks up a black binder off the table and flips through the contents. His hand twitches with each page he turns. I grab a chair next to Charles.

"Let's start the meeting, Troy," Nurse Lisa says.

The beard shouts, "Quiet everyone. Our Community meeting will come to order. Let me start out by reading our patient rules and responsibilities.

One. Patients shall not engage in any physical or verbal acts of aggression against either other patients or staff." His voice fades as billows of dense fog start to drift across the room.

"Two. Patients shall not engage in any overt acts of a sexual nature with either other patients or staff."

The fog swallows his legs, then his arms, leaving only his decapitated beard which bobs above the mist.

"Three. Patients shall not consume any alcohol or drugs except those dispensed by the clinic staff for therapeutic purposes."

His beard sinks under and I drift off.

I'd rather die than hurt Christy.

CHAPTER 5

"Erik, your turn," Nurse Lisa says.

I strain to read the whiteboard across the room. "My mood is depressed and my goal is to make it through the day."

"More like stay awake," the pirate calls out.

"Give him a break," Charles says. "It's his first day. He's still getting use to his meds."

"No criticism of other people's feelings or goals," Nurse Lisa says. "Let's wrap this up, Troy. It's time to start therapy groups."

Across the room, the beard rises from his chair: "I hereby bring this Community meeting to a close. Remember that whatever happens here or you hear here, stays here."

He pounds the table with his fist. A loud chorus erupts across the room, "Hear, hear!" the patients shout back in unison. The sound reverberates off the concrete walls like the closing "Amen" of a church revival meeting.

I turn to Charles, "Where now?"

"We have ACT class this morning."

I limp off, rubbing my left knee.

Entering the classroom, I realize there's no place to hide. All the chairs are placed along three perimeter walls and face inward. The chairs are black bucket seats with chrome limbs, splayed out like spider legs onto the grey carpet. Along one wall a row of windows looks out on an empty parking lot.

Patients are seated around the room in various states of slumber. The air is muggy. Along the open wall there's a large whiteboard and a short, wiry man wearing tweed pants, a beige dress shirt and a maroon tie. He wipes the board clean with a rag. I slink into an empty chair in the far corner.

The man turns to address the class. His curly brown hair is receding over a prominent brow and thick rimmed glasses. "Good morning," he says in a bass voice.

"Good morning, Mr. Carson," the patients say. Their off-key voices clank in my head.

"Today I ask, what you want out of life? How about you, Erik?"

"Right now, I'd settle for a new body, this model is high mileage."

"How about you, Alex?" Carson asks.

The pirate pauses, squinting his eyes. "I'd like a Tesla and a million dollars," he says with a smirk. "Then I'd be ready to **paarrty**," Alex shouts as he shimmies his arms and hips in a frenzy without leaving his chair.

Carson grins. "What prevents us from finding happiness?" he asks.

He turns and faces a young blond, who squirms in her seat. She wears pink "Hello Kitty" pajamas and matching nail polish. Her face is pale and thin, but she's cute. Her fingernails are chewed off, a kitten with no claws.

"Sandy, are you happy?"

"No," she says. She looks up at Carson briefly but shifts her gaze away.

The floor starts to sink. No one else in the room seems to notice. I grab the seat of my chair.

"Why not?"

"My father died."

The edges of the hole spill like water down a drain.

Carson pauses, his face softens, "I'm sorry to hear that."

I watch my legs, my chest, get swallowed and disappear.

I'm falling down the rabbit hole.

Sandy slides back in her chair and chews on a few strands of her blond hair.

"Humans experience the loss of loved ones, old age and death," Carson says. "It's beyond our control."

With one last gasp of air, I'm sucked under.

Have I lost Christy?

CHAPTER 6

Carson stands in front of me. He wipes his damp forehead with a handkerchief embroidered with the letters CG. "Erik, class is over. I didn't have the heart to wake you."

"Sorry."

"Remember we only have a short time to patch you up in here," he says, patting me on the shoulder. He turns and walks out the door, leaving me to clear the stupor from my head.

I hobble back to my room. My bed has been made with fresh linens and a small packet of papers sits on my dresser. I see from the inpatient program schedule I have an hour of Leisure/Education Activity. My mouth is parched but I'm too exhausted to walk into the bath room for water. I crawl back under the covers wearing all my clothes and gaze up at the ceiling tiles.

My thoughts were no longer under my control. I'd hear Christy drive off to work and be overwhelmed with loneliness. I knew it was foolish to feel abandoned by such a trivial separation. She would never abandon me, or would she? I crawled back under the sheets and wept. The serpent brought me to my knees. "I'll do anything you want," I whisper, "just make the pain go away." He wrapped himself around me and squeezed even harder.

You've screwed up the best thing in your life. You're worthless!

I hear the door open and to see Charles lope into the room.

"Erik, get up. You'll miss lunch."

I've been out cold for two and a half hours.

I follow Charles to the dining room. He points to an empty chair, then grabs my tray from the food cart.

At the table, Alex wolfs down a hamburger stuffed with French fries stacked between two thin buns. Taking a huge bite, several fries smothered in ketchup flop onto his tray.

A long limbed thirty-year-old walks up to the table. "Room for one more?" she asks in a throaty voice. She sits down on the opposite side of the table. "Who's the new guy?"

"Gina, this is Erik," Charles says.

She extends a hand across the table. I tip over my coffee as a snake tattoo rears its head from under her sleeve. She smiles. Alex spits up another French fry.

"You weren't at class, Erik," Alex says.

"I fell asleep."

"Better ask Dr. Williams to cut back on your meds," Alex says.

"You'll be fine," Gina says. "It took me three days to get used to my meds."

"Glad to hear I'm not the first," I say.

"How are the burgers over at the prison?" Alex asks.

"They serve a tasty bacon and cheese burger," she says, spreading mustard across the open bun. I wonder what Gina did to end up in prison.

Alex wipes the last drop of ketchup from his plate with a French fry and looks up. "I lost my high school sweetheart to a hamburger," he says.

"What?" I ask.

"She was a vegetarian. If I ate meat, she wouldn't bump uglies."

"You're kidding," I say.

"No, she was a real vegetotalitarian," he says. "I only lasted one month. I broke down and ate a Big Mac one night on the way to her house. She dumped me that night."

"How'd she know?" I ask.

"One kiss," Alex says.

Nurse Lisa's brassy voice breaks in over the loudspeaker. "There will be a fifteen-minute cigarette break out on the smoking lawn in five minutes." The table bustles with activity. In two minutes, I'm alone. It reminds me of a fire drill, except everyone here races toward the flames.

CHAPTER 7

"Go get some rest," says Charles, as he wipes down the adjoining table.

"I thought you were going out for a smoke," I say.

"I'm cutting back. It's part of the new me."

"I'm trying to find the old me."

He smiles. Despite his weathered exterior, Charles is growing on me. I'd want him in my corner in a title fight. Halfway down the hall I stop to look over the tattered books piled on a shelf along the wall: *Managing Depression*, *The Twelve Steps of Alcoholics Anonymous*, *The Holy Bible (The King James Version)* and *Jurassic Park*. I almost pick up *Managing Depression* but decide I'm too depressed to deal with my depression right now. I grab the *Twelve Steps* and head to my room.

The smell of stale sweat floods my nose as I enter the room. I try to open the window but it's locked tight. My in-patient program schedule says I've missed the exercise break and I'm late for my art therapy class. I'm not feeling artsy-craftsy. I crawl into bed and open up *The Twelve Steps of Alcoholics Anonymous*. This is an odd choice, since I don't drink, but decide it could come in handy if I ever start. As I read, my mind replays a sliver of a dream, a nightmare, actually. I'm being dragged to the side of a road as cars scream past. The picture won't stay in focus. The book drops from my hands.

Mom will be devastated when she finds out where I am.

• • •

"It's time for evening wrap up." Nurse Lisa shouts across the room.

The inmates assemble. Troy recites his rules of decorum.

"How did you do today, Sandy?" Nurse Lisa asks. There's a mustard stain dribbled across the "Hello Kitty" on her chest.

"I felt better after lunch. I ate four bites of my hamburger."

"That's a good start." The gallery nods and a polite round of applause sounds around the room.

"How was your first day, Erik?" Dr. Williams asks.

"I'm still here."

"What did you think of your classes?"

"OK."

"And how are you feeling?"

"Still depressed."

"Well, you've met your goal for today. It's a first step."

Chapter 8

After breakfast Dr. Williams strides into my room wearing cargo pants and a green golf shirt under his lab coat. "Your wife called last night. You were sound asleep. She said she'd call back tonight after six."

"What did she say?"

"She told the nurse to tell you she's OK."

I flash to the vows Christy and I shared on the beach in Hawaii. "In sickness and in health… to have and to hold… as long as we both shall live." The tropical breeze flows across the sand and warms my chest. Dr. Williams sits down across from me.

"How did you sleep?"

"I was out cold for ten hours and my mouth is bone dry."

"That's a common side effect," he says. A small alligator is visible on his chest beneath his white coat. "Drink a lot of water. It gets easier as your body adjusts." He flips through the papers in a manila file. "I see from your records this is your first treatment for a mental health issue."

I look down at Dr. Williams' canvas loafers. His socks have gone AWOL again.

"I haven't slept much lately," I say.

"Why not?"

"It's everything: my mom, work, my bum knee, bad back."

He leans forward. "Talk to me about it."

"Where do I start?"

"How about your knee and back?"

I cross my arms. "Talking about it won't help."

"I'm here when you're ready." He taps me on the knee.

"At times I think I'm losing it."

"What do you mean by losing it?"

"I'm just going through a rough patch," I say, rubbing the back of my neck.

"Can you describe your rough patch?"

"I already did."

"You're sad." He writes some notes in my file.

"Wouldn't anyone whose mom is dying be upset?"

"Tell me about your feelings?"

There's a minute of awkward silence.

"Ok. How long have you felt like this?"

"A couple of months."

"Once the Prozac kicks in those feelings will fade. It takes a few weeks, so don't get discouraged. It looks like the Seroquel is getting you into a healthy sleep pattern."

"How long do I take these drugs?"

"Some patients take medication for the rest of their lives. I've had others stop after one month and never look back. Everyone's different."

"One month's not bad."

"Don't get ahead of yourself."

"I won't."

I'll be off this in a week.

"Grab me any time," he says, turning to walk out the door.

CHAPTER 9

I sit down next to Charles who shows Sandy how to play drums with two pencils on an empty coffee cup. Gina is curled up in her chair, half-asleep. Alex walks in holding his stomach like he's ready to redecorate the carpet with his breakfast. Carson stands at the front of the class, waiting for Alex to find a seat. He's wearing grey pinstriped slacks, a white dress shirt and dark blue tie. With his receding hair line and black rimmed glasses, he looks the part of a college professor.

"Alex, how do you cope with suffering?" Carson asks.

"Alcohol is my drug of choice."

"And how's that strategy working?"

"Lousy, I'm stuck in here."

"Can you suffer and still be happy?" asks Carson.

"You can't," Alex says.

"A woman giving birth experiences both intense pain and joy," Carson says.

"You want me to push a bowling ball out my ass and enjoy it?" says Alex.

"Nothing so daunting," Carson says.

"I don't get it," I say.

"What are you thinking about right this instant?" Carson asks me.

"I wish my wife was here."

"But she isn't."

"Obviously."

"And how does that make you feel?"

"Anxious."

"You're wishing things were different from what they are?"

"I guess."

"That's resistance. Focus on right here, right now."

If this "woo-woo" stuff is what it takes to get out, I'm in. "OK," I say.

"Gina, are you inside your head or focused on the outside world?" Carson asks.

No answer.

"Gina, are you IN or OUT?" Carson says.

Sandy shakes Gina's arm. Gina unconsciously slaps her hand away and lets out a short moan. Sandy tosses up her hands in surrender. Carson stands at attention, like the honor guard at the Tomb of the Unknown Soldier.

My eye catches an old man in a wheelchair in a mad dash across the parking lot outside. He pushes the hand wheels on his chair as fast as he can, wearing white diapers and white socks, nothing else. The wispy white hair on his bare chest reminds me of a plucked chicken.

Finally, Gina stirs from her stupor. "What did you ask?"

Carson lets a smile slowly emerge. "Humans have sixty thousand thoughts per day. Eighty percent are repeats and negative. We replay the same old tapes in our brain like a TV soap opera. Gina, what were you thinking a moment ago?"

"I need to get off my lazy ass and get back to work."

"If you were renting a room in your brain and your roommate said that, what would you do?"

Gina rubs her arm for a moment. "I'd tell him to get lost."

"I'd do the same," Carson says. "Everyone, close your eyes and concentrate on your breath. Focus on the air flowing through your nose. As you breathe in, say, 'May you be happy,' and as you breathe out, 'May you find peace.'"

Now we're chanting like a group of Hare Krishna.

Alex points out the window. The wheelchair disappears from my view just as two young nurses in blue scrubs appear, running across the tarmac in pursuit, their arms waving in the air.

"It's an escapee from the geriatric ward of the hospital next door." Alex whispers. "They never make it far."

"You may get an itch or your mind may wander." Carson says. "Don't suppress your sensations or thoughts. Step back and observe. Now gently focus on your breath and repeat the words."

The room falls silent except for the soft whisperings of "May you be happy, may you find peace," and the sound of Gina snoring.

I wonder if she's thinking of me…Stay focused…*She hates me*…Breath in… *I'm stuck in a loony bin*…Breath out…*I'm screwed*…Breath in…*I wonder if the Buddha ever got depressed*…Focus you dipshit… I suck at this.

• • •

The herd lumbers out the door. I join the migration.

"I don't get this new age meditation BS," Alex says, walking down the hall. "I can't sit and do nothing."

"It reminds me of prayer, but you don't talk." Sandy says.

"It's mumbo jumbo," Alex says. "Completely useless."

"I don't know why they call it mindfulness if you're supposed to empty all the crap out of your head," I say.

"It should be called mindlessness," Alex says.

"Listen for the voice inside your head," Charles says.

"That guy is an asshole," says Alex. "He always rants and raves."

"Just let him," Charles says. "Eventually he shuts up."

"Not mine," Alex says.

"That's why we get those little pink pills every morning," Gina says, "to shut the jerk up."

Alex laughs, leading us into the recreation room.

I sit down next to Charles in the corner and watch him put pen to paper.

"What are you writing?" I ask.

"A letter to my wife. I'm thanking her for putting up with my sorry ass."

"She's been supportive?"

"She's a saint." He scribbles a few words and then crosses them out. "I'm trying to explain why I keep ending up in here."

"Why's that?"

"This is the only place I fit in."

"This place scares me," I say.

"In here I can talk to anyone about anything," Charles says. "Nothing is off limits."

"So, you like pouring out your guts to Dr. Williams and Carson?"

"I share my baggage with them, but I get more from the other patients. We've been through it."

"I could never do that," I say. I can't let anyone inside. They'll see I'm a wimp. I can't control my feelings anymore. I sat on the couch and cried last week. What kind of a man does that?

Charles tips his bald head and stares at me over the top of his reading glasses.

CHAPTER 10

Nurse Lisa and two burly attendants escort a new patient into the clinic, one orderly on each side: a short middle-aged man with a stout barrel chest and young man wearing a cross on a string around his neck.

"That's Maru," Charles says. "He's Samoan. The older one is Eli. He's Basque. He can pin a sheep with his left hand and sheer it with his right."

The patient wedged between them has a sun baked face and a scruffy beard. He wears tattered jeans, a greasy denim jacket and grimy tennis shoes. A crusty black toenail pokes out of one shoe. His bloodshot eyes flash the look of a wild animal.

"That guy smells like road kill," I say.

"That's Larry," Charles says. "He's been here before."

"Is he violent?" Gina asks.

"He's homeless and schizophrenic," Charles says. "Last time he slept all day and roamed the halls at night, never went to a single class."

Daniel had a jacket like that when he was homeless. Mom begged him to come home with her. He didn't want to be a burden on her.

"His brain's fried," Alex says. "They're wasting their time."

They beat Daniel to a pulp for that jacket. I should have dragged him off the mean streets.

Nurse Lisa leaves Larry and approaches our table. Everyone stops eating and looks up.

"Erik, can you move into Charles' room, so we can give our new patient his own place? I don't want him to keep a roommate awake at night."

"Shall I move my stuff now?"

"That would be great," Nurse Lisa says, turning her attention back to the new patient.

"I'll give you a hand," Charles says. We walk off to my room.

• • •

Charles and I carry clothes and toiletries down the hall to my new home past Nurse Lisa. "You know the rules, Larry. You need to take a shower and put on some clean clothes as part of the admittance process." She holds a fresh pair of blue hospital scrubs, a shower head and a pair of white flip flops in her hands. Maru and Eli flank Larry, who stares at Lisa for a long minute. Maru sets his hand on Larry's shoulder. Larry grabs the clothes and snorts, "Aargh" and some other drivel and then he walks towards his bathroom. I'm pretty sure I hear the word "bitch," but Nurse Lisa turns and walks away.

"Never pick a fight with Maru," says Charles. "He was a defensive lineman in college, played for Alabama. Might have gone into the pros if he hadn't torn his ACL."

"I'd take him on before I'd pick a fight with Nurse Lisa," I say.

"Got that right," Charles says.

Chapter 11

Charles room is a mirror image of my own, except it's nicer. It has a rosy glow. Maybe he has better insurance coverage. I dump all my clothes on top of the cream-colored dresser and sit down.

"I grew up in Southern California," I say, "and my mom still lives in Pasadena."

"Jackie Robinson's home town," says Charles. "Where do you want your toothbrush and stuff?"

I point to the top on the dresser. "Dump it there. I played a couple of little league games on Jackie Robinson field when I was a kid."

"Dodgers could use a base runner like him right now. I had season tickets, but had to give them up."

"What happened?" I ask, folding my clothes.

"I lost my job and then they took our house."

He was crushed by the recession, just like me.

I sit down on the bed across from Charles. He stares at the floor and rubs his bald head with his leathery palms.

"Never felt so useless in my life."

I pick up a loose sock off the floor and toss it on the dresser. *At least we're still making the house payments.*

"I'm lost without my work," I say.

"You know, then."

He seems honest, a hard worker.

"I'll never retire. I'd go crazy."

"I tried to commit suicide last week." I lean back on the bed and stare up at the tan ceiling tiles. Never thought I'd say that.

"I thought about it," Charles says, "but I could never do that to my wife and son." He puts one hand up to his chin and drops the other onto his knee, like Rodin's *The Thinker*.

Suddenly, I don't want to talk about it.

Nurse Patty, the keyboard pianist, sticks her head inside the door, the short curls in her red hair bounce like springs around her face.

"Sorry to interrupt, Dr. Williams needs to talk to you, Mr. Brown."

"OK," Charles says.

I watch as he lumbers down the hall. He's just a regular guy with a methamphetamine problem.

• • •

Half an hour later, I'm out in the game room when Charles reappears.

"My grandfather's back in the hospital." he says.

"Most people don't appreciate their parents, till it's too late, Sandy says, looking up from her journal. Losing Mom is forcing me to face my own mortality.

I look over her shoulder.

"What are you writing?" I ask.

"A letter to my father." The words are damp, dripping off the page. Full of longing and affection.

I never knew my dad. He died when I was five.

"I thought he passed away?" Gina says.

"Carson suggested I write him, tell him the things I never got to say before he died." There are other words. Sharp ones. The kind that sever ligaments and tendons.

I remember Dad yelled at Mom.

"Were you close?" Gina asks.

"He divorced my mom when I was a teenager and moved to Kentucky. I spent my summers with him, riding horses." The words are jumbled together, rocks in a blender. It's loud. The pages weep.

Mom never cried though. She was tough as nails.

"He owned horses?" John asks.

"He was a jockey. That's how he died; his horse shattered a leg and collapsed." Sandy's eyes are swollen with tears.

Women are too emotional.

The last page is soothing. The words whisper with forgiveness.

"At least he died doing something he enjoyed," Charles says.

"I'd give anything to have ten minutes with him."

I need to see my mom before I lose her.

Sandy closes her diary. The sobs fade away.

"I'm sure he's listening," Charles says. "The Lakota believe the spirit of a loved one lingers for a year. They have a rite to purify the soul of the dead. It increases our love for one another."

"Are you part Indian?" Gina asks.

"I'm one quarter Lakota."

"What's it called?" Sandy asks.

"Wanagi Wicagluha. In English it's 'the keeping of the spirit.'"

"That's beautiful," says Sandy.

CHAPTER 12

Larry watches TV, sprawled out on the couch like a lizard. Charles and Troy, the beard, sit on chairs nearby. The nightly news is on, but Larry turned the volume off.

I tap Larry on the leg.

"Got room for one more?" I ask.

Larry delivers a quick kick to my leg. "Don't touch me!" Larry says.

"Ouch," I say, stepping back to rub my shin. "Don't be such a jerk!"

Maru suddenly appears and puts his imposing Samoan frame between me and Larry. "No violence," he says.

"Fuck off!" Larry shouts. Larry takes a wild round house swing at Maru who catches Larry's arm and then drags him off towards the counseling room.

"Are you OK?" Charles asks.

"I'm fine." I say.

"Larry's a powder keg," Troy says. "They should lock him up and throw away the key."

I decide it's best to steer clear of Larry and walk down the hall to check the phones. I don't belong with these crazy people.

Two phones hang on the wall by the bookshelf. The line for outgoing calls looks like the queue for porta potties at the Boston Marathon half an hour before the start. The incoming phone stares at me in silence.

"Come on, Gina," Alex says, squirming.

"I'll be done in a minute," she says, sharing a laugh with the other end of her call.

Suddenly, she shouts, "Screw you!" and slams down the phone. Her black leather boots stomp away, leaving the room silent.

This place is a madhouse.

"Women should come with warning labels," Alex says.

"How so?" I ask.

"Highly flammable. Keep from open flames or may blow up in your face," Alex says.

"Or cleaning instructions, at a minimum," Alex says. "Wash separately in cold water or colors may bleed, along with your nose."

The phone rings. I freeze. Alex picks it up. "It's your wife."

The phone slips off my fingers. It dangles, clanking off the block wall twice before I snatch it back. My hand shakes.

"Hi honey, how are you?" I croak.

Her voice is ice cubes. "They kept me at the hospital for two days."

I start to sob. "I am so sorry."

"How could you do that?"

"I can't remember."

The patients in line turn away. I'm humiliated.

"You're lying," she says.

I lower my voice. "Ask the doctor."

"You expect me to believe you forgot the worst day of my life."

"Tell me what I did." Alex brings me a chair. I sit down.

"You're an asshole," she says.

Christy never swears.

"Tell me what I did!" I cover my eyes with one hand.

"You don't want to know."

"I don't want to lose you."

The line is silent. I wipe the tears off my cheek.

"I'll do whatever it takes to make it up," I say.

"I'm never going through this again."

I take a deep breath. "You won't. I promise."

"You need to get fixed and fast."

"I will."

"So, they're helping you."

"I'm already better."

"Are you really?" She sighs.

"I'm learning to meditate."

"Erik, you have the attention span of a four-year-old." She used my name, not *a-hole*.

"You're right. I need to work on that."

"Well, **that's** a first."

"What, what did I say?"

"You didn't argue when I criticized you."

"I admit, I'm not perfect." *I'd better get used to this.*

"Can I get that in writing? I want to put it on the refrigerator."

"I'll write down all my faults, if you want," I say, "but we'll need a bigger refrigerator."

"What are they feeding you in there?" she asks.

"They serve a lot of humble pie."

"Are you going to start cooking and cleaning up the kitchen?" Christy asks.

"I'll help around the kitchen a lot more than I have. I know that."

"I want to speak to Erik Scott, apparently someone else picked up the phone."

"I'll change, honey." Don't let her go till she promises to visit.

"How do I know that?" Christy asks.

"Come visit. I'll show you."

"You do sound more agreeable."

"You mean the world to me," I say. *I'll be paying this off for years.*

We talk for the next twenty minutes. I figure out a dozen ways to say I'm a dipshit and I'm sorry. I still feel her connection. It's the sliver of light that flickers through the rubble of my collapsed life.

She tells me she'll come for family visitation day.

I tell her I love her.

She hangs up without a response.

Chapter 13

I walk out to the courtyard where the smokers are finishing up their nightly convention. "Larry's an asshole," I mumble, rubbing my bruised shin.

"Don't let him get you," Charles says. "It's not worth it."

"Somebody needs to teach him a lesson," Alex says.

"Don't feed the wolf," Charles says to me.

"What?" I ask.

"It's a Cherokee fable: a young boy, angry at another boy, came to his grandfather. The grandfather listened, then said, 'Hate eats at you and does nothing to your enemy. It's like taking poison and wishing your enemy would die. It's as if we have two wolves living inside us. One is good and lives in harmony with others. He does not take offense when none is intended. He will only fight when it is right to do so. But the other wolf fights everyone, all the time, for no reason. The smallest thing will send him into a fury, but his anger doesn't change anything. It's helpless anger. It's hard to live with two wolves inside us. Both try to dominate our spirits.'

'Which wolf wins?' the boy asked.

'The one I feed,' said the grandfather."

"So, Erik's supposed to let Larry get away with this?" Alex says.

"It's not about Larry," Charles says.

"What will they do with him?" Sandy asks.

"They'll put him in an outpatient program," says Charles, "but he'll probably end up back in the woods."

At least I have a roof over my head.

"That's the Big Dipper," Charles says, pointing to a cluster of stars. "The stars of the Big Dipper signify the Seven Council Fires, each one represents one of the tribes that form the Great Sioux Nation."

"The stars remind me how insignificant I am," I say.

"We're all part of the universe," Charles says.

I'm surrounded by people, but I feel all alone in here.

• • •

I meet with Carson later that morning.

"Come in," he says when I knock on the door to the counseling office. There are two desks in the room on adjoining walls. Mary's desk is cluttered with files, books and wood framed pictures of her family surrounding a computer monitor and keyboard. Carson's desk is larger and completely empty, except for a white laptop computer, a phone and a Rubik's Cube, all six sides a separate color, sitting alone in the far corner.

"What can I do for you?" Carson asks.

"My wife called me last night."

While leaning back in his chair, Carson pulls off his maroon red tie and unties the top button on his dress shirt. "How did it go?"

"She didn't believe me when I told her I couldn't remember my suicide attempt."

"Have you lied to her before?"

I don't answer.

He slips off his brown oxfords, stretching out his legs under his desk. His big toe sticks out a hole in his left sock.

"Well, you can understand, she'll have trust issues being alone with you."

Christy would never let me wear socks like that.

"What should I do?" I ask.

"Talk to her. Make her feel safe."

I pause and rub my forehead. "I'll work on that."

"I can meet with you and Christy to talk things over, if you want."

"She's coming for visitation tomorrow morning."

"I'll set aside some time."

"OK, but I need to ask her. Can I make a call?"

"Sure," says Carson, nodding towards the phone.

I dial Christy and say, "Hi, honey."

"How are you?" she asks.

"I'm talking with a therapist right now and he suggested we meet with him tomorrow for a counseling session. Would that be OK?"

There's a moment of silence. "I guess so," she whispers.

"Thanks, honey," I say. "I love you."

"Okay," she says and hangs up. I nod to Carson. "She'll be here."

Carson slips his shoes back on. "Good. We'll meet here tomorrow at 10:30."

I stand up to leave but stop and pick up the Rubik's Cube. "I used to own one of these. I never did figure it out. How long did it take you?"

"I've had that on my desk for years. Mary said one of the patients fiddled with it last night. When he left, she noticed all the outside faces were a matching color."

"Who was it?" I ask.

"Larry."

Chapter 14

After dinner, Charles picks out a board game from the bookshelf and sets it in the middle of the table. "Anyone want to play the Game of Life?" he calls out.

Gina walks over to our table. "Would you read this for us?" Charles asks, handing Gina the instructions.

Sandy and Alex pull up chairs. Charles sets up the board. Gina reads the directions in a slow, earthy tone. "Each player should pick a car and fit a people peg into the driver's seat. Don't forget to buckle up."

As everyone reaches for their game markers, I grab a green car and drop a pink peg in the front seat.

"Wrong color, Erik" Charles says.

"What?"

"Pink is for girls," Charles says. "Unless you're a switch hitter you need to use the blue peg."

"Gotcha," I say, quickly exchanging my pink one for a blue.

"Everyone's got to play by the rules," Charles mumbles.

Gina continues reading from the book. "All players spin the wheel. Highest spinner takes the first turn. Play then continues clockwise."

We each take a spin of the wheel. On his first attempt, Alex hurls the plastic wheel across the table.

A swing and a miss.

"Careful there, Brutus," Charles says. "Don't break the wheel before we start.

Alex gives it a second try. The wheel flies off the table and crashes on the floor. "Damn, this is harder than it looks."

"Nobody said this was going to be easy," Charles says. He crawls under the table to retrieve the wheel. On his third attempt, Alex manages to keep the roulette wheel from spinning out of control.

We each take our turn.

"Charles, seven is the high number. You're first," Gina says.

Charles lands on a payday and becomes a lawyer. Alex becomes a veterinarian and then picks up an action card that reads, "Fired for sneaking your cat into work."

"That's BS!" Alex shouts. "I'm an animal doctor."

Gina checks the rule book. "Sorry, Alex, pick a new career."

"Hasbro's screwed me!" he says.

Charles calls it corporate malfeasance.

Forty minutes into the "Game of Life" and the whole table is a disaster. Alex chases the wheel across the floor for the seventh time. Sandy cries because she ended up with twins after she admits she really doesn't want kids. Gina and Charles argue over whether Gina can buy homeowners insurance for her Victorian mansion two spins after she bought it. I try to keep track of the bank money, but I can't figure out the interest on our loans without the calculator on my phone.

The *Game of Life* has reduced us to shambles.

Chapter 15

I wait for my wife and brother to arrive, sitting at attention like a dog waiting for its owner to toss a ball. The visitation room bustles with nervous anticipation as the lucky patients expecting family and friends rehearse their upcoming conversations. Troy stands in a corner, mumbling to himself. Alex writes notes on a pad and then furiously erases them. Charles talks to Eli at the nursing station. I look down the hall to see Sandy sitting, dejected, on the couch in the TV lounge, like a kid passed over when the soccer teams are picked.

Looking up, I catch sight of Joe and Christy walking down the entrance hall. Joe wears his usual pin striped grey business suit and black leather oxfords. He's carrying a small laptop briefcase. Christy is well dressed, as always, in dark blue slacks and a matching three quarter length sleeve jacket. Joe's hand is on Christy's shoulder, and he whispers in her ear. She wears large black sunglasses and her blond hair is swept to one side, exposing a bandage by her left eye.

Did I do that to her?

As the guard opens the door, Joe steps forward and gives me a bear hug.

"It's good to see you, brother," he says.

Clinging to Joe, I feel Christy's fingers touch my back.

"It's great to see both of you," I say. "You have no idea how much this means to me."

Joe moves aside. Christy tries to smile, but the lines in her face are stretched taut with tension. We share a clumsy embrace; her hands pat my shoulder like she's petting a strange dog. She steps back.

"You are so lucky to be married to this woman," Joe says. "Most wives would be filing divorce papers at the courthouse right now."

I break into tears. Christy hugs me briefly, her face contorted with pain.

"Let's find a place to sit down," Joe says. I buck up and dry my tears.

"There's an empty couch in the corner," Christy says, pointing across the room. I sit in the middle of the couch with Christy on my left and Joe on my right. Joe lands a sharp blow on my right shoulder. It's the exact spot I hit him when we were kids.

"How are you?" Joe asks.

"Better, I'm taking sleep medication and a happy pill. How's Mom?"

"They've stopped the chemo," Joe says. "The cancer's spread. It's in her lungs and stomach. She's been asking about you. She wondered why you didn't call last week."

"You haven't told her where I am, have you?"

"I told her you were off on a consulting job and forgot to call."

There's an awkward moment of silence.

"I'll let you two talk," Joe says and stands up. "Is there drinking water around here?"

"There's ice water and paper cups in the next room."

"I'll get three," Joe says. He walks away.

I put my hand on her knee; her muscles tense. I pull my hand back.

Stay calm.

"What you did…" she says.

"I screwed up. I hurt you."

She folds her arms, looking down at the floor. "You hurt us."

My palms are sweaty, my mouth chalk dry. "I thought you'd be better off without me."

"How could you think that?"

"I didn't want to ruin our marriage." Christy looks up. Her eyes slice me in two.

"So, you thought you'd off yourself and leave me all alone."

"You're the best thing in my life. I was afraid I'd bring you down with me."

Christy shakes her head. "You are clueless Erik Scott."

"Yes, I was," I say, rubbing my hands on my pant legs.

She's not going to let me off easy.

"And self-centered," she says.

"That too."

I deserve every punch she throws at me.

"Why didn't you tell me how you felt?"

"I'm supposed to be strong."

She points her finger at me. "You should have talked to me."

"I was too numb."

Christy shakes her head. "That's why you should open up."

She doesn't understand. Talking won't fix it. I have to bear down and ride this out.

"I thought you'd leave me."

"After thirty-two years together?" she says.

I doubted Christy. I doubted myself.

Joe walks back into the room. “Good to see you two talking,” he says. He gives us each a cup of water. I wash down my remorse with a gulp of water.

Carson approaches from across the room.

“Carson, this is Christy,” I say, standing up.

“Nice to meet you,” he says. They shake hands. Christy smiles weakly.

“And my brother Joe.”

“My pleasure,” Joe says. “You can take whatever time you need for your meeting. I’ve got emails to write.” He pulls out his laptop.

“Shall we?” Carson says, leading us down to his office.

Chapter 16

"Make yourselves comfortable," he says, pointing to two chairs in front of his desk. He takes his seat behind it. "Do you want some coffee?"

"No thanks," Christy says.

"How are you doing?" Carson asks Christy. She taps her foot on the carpet.

"I'm still in shock."

"That's a natural reaction."

Her hands clutch the seat cushion. "I've been trying to stay composed. I get upset when I think about it."

"Erik's told me a little about what happened, but I'd like to hear it from you, if you're comfortable talking about it."

I don't want to hear this.

OK," Christy says. She holds her right index fingers over her lips for a long minute. "He was sick in bed this winter with pneumonia and his bad back. His orthopedic surgeon said he may need surgery on his knee." She runs her fingers through her hair. "Normally he runs to relieve stress, but he could barely get out of bed."

I've never felt like that before, feeble and petrified.

"And how were you and Erik getting along?"

"In the past we turned to one another when things got rough, but this was different. I was losing him. Losing us."

I was hollow inside.

"Explain rough," Carson says.

"He stopped sharing, stopped talking to me."

I'll talk about anything you want, just don't leave me.

"Is that the way it felt to you, Erik?" Carson asks.

I felt gutted.

"I didn't want to drag Christy through my misery," I say, rubbing the back of my neck.

Why would I do that? I love my wife.

"Describe what you were going through," Carson asks.

My body ached. My brain spun in circles of self-torture. I was all alone. *She's better off without me.*

"I hadn't slept for six or seven days."

"How could that be?" Christy says. "We were in the same bed."

"You never told Christy you weren't sleeping?"

"No." It would just upset her.

"Was Erik ever aggressive?" Carson asks.

My heart starts to race.

"Never," she pauses, biting her lip. "Except…" She starts to cry.

She's never going to forgive me.

Carson hands her a tissue. "…the day we ended up in the hospital."

I'm humiliated. I would never hit my wife.

"I know this is hard," Carson says.

Tell me what I did.

"I can't talk about it." Christy says. She wipes the tears from her cheek.

"That wasn't Erik. After thirty-two years of marriage I know that."

"It's been well documented that after three days without sleep, healthy people develop psychotic symptoms," Carson says. "Seven days would result in a complete psychotic breakdown."

I had insomnia. I'm not psychotic. Don't shame me.

"I'm sleeping much better now."

"That's important. You can't let that happen to you again."

"I won't. I promise."

"Erik has been making good progress," Carson says, "but it will take time for him to heal." I've gone to every one of your therapy sessions.

"Is he safe to be around?" I did everything you asked me to do.

I've learned my lesson. I won't crumble like that again.

"He's much calmer than when he first arrived, but why don't you ask him?"

I'm better.

"Is it safe for me to go home with you?" she asks. Her face is etched with lines of doubt.

I'll be fine.

"I won't hurt you ever again," I say, dropping my head in my hands.

Please take me back.

"You've been very understanding, given the circumstances." Carson says. "I'm sure Erik appreciates that."

"I do," I stammer.

"I don't know if I want to hit him over the head with a club or make him chicken soup."

"Soup sounds good," I say.

Christy's face softens and she puts her hand on my knee. "I won't give up on my husband." Carson smiles across the desk.

We're going to be OK. I need to go home.

"Can I be released?" I ask. Christy looks at Carson.

I want to hold her in my arms.

"Technically, we can't hold you after seventy-two hours," Carson says, "but I recommend you stay for additional therapy."

"Can I take therapy outside the clinic?" I'll do whatever you want. Just let me go free.

"I do private counseling two days a week."

"Sign me up."

"You'll also need a psychiatrist to manage your medication. Do you have one?"

"No."

I'll get you an appointment with Dr. Reed. He's the only local doctor taking on new patients."

"What do you think, honey?" I ask.

"I don't know."

Make her feel safe.

"I'll meet with Carson and Dr. Reed."

I'll take whatever pills they want.

"Do you promise?"

I won't miss a session.

"I promise."

Christy is silent.

"I'll sleep upstairs in the guest bedroom, till you decide otherwise," I say.

Christy gazes at her tissue.

"I'll ask Joe to stay with us," I say.

"Are you sure he can do that?"

"Let's ask," I say.

Three hours later, I'm officially released.

I'm OK, now. I'll show her.

PART TWO

"I can't explain myself," said Alice,
"because I'm not myself, you see."[3]

Chapter 17

Walking out of the clinic into the bright sunshine, a sense of freedom overwhelms me. I'd been locked up for three long days. The sky is an intense shade of blue and light wispy clouds curl off the top of Snow Peak like strands of hair that dance in the wind. The swollen buds of a cottonwood tree infuse the air with the scent of pine and honey. The concrete walkway leading out of the clinic is lined with strips of closely cropped grass that surround two rhododendron bushes bursting with pink flowers. Even the broad expanse of the parking lot is a welcome sight compared to the stark block walls that caged me.

"Hold up," I say, dropping Christy's hand to pull off my shoes and socks.

"What are you doing?" Joe asks.

"Stopping to smell the roses," I say, squeezing the fresh cut blades of grass between my toes.

Suddenly I'm knocked off my feet by a frenzied black fireball of fur with a tail wagging at warp speed.

"Cash, it's good to see you too, buddy," I say, rubbing my nose in his face.

"I told you he would never stay in the truck bed," Christy says with a smile.

Joe shrugs his shoulders.

"You look tired," Cash says, licking my chin.

I jump three feet backwards and land sprawled out on the lawn.

"Are you OK?" Joe says, helping me up.

A gorilla hoots and howls inside my skull; my ears rings and mind spins. I can't let them know I'm hearing voices.

"Doggy breath," I say, waving my hand in front of my nose. They'll lock me back up.

"Better get Cash some dental biscuits," Joe says.

Cash sits looking at me, as if nothing happened. I'm nauseous.

Christy gives me a quizzical look, *Are you sure you're OK?*

"Joe and I will get the car," she says.

Joe whispers to Christy as they walk to the car. They think I'm a basket case. I have to hold myself together.

"Thanks, honey," I say and sit down in the grass. "Give me a minute to slip on my shoes and socks.

Cash trots up to me. "Christy's worried about you," he says.

The gorilla in my skull screeches and pounds his chest, battering my temples.

"It's just a passing hallucination," I say, putting on my shoes. Cash rubs his nose on my knee.

I push him away and practically run to the truck. "You sure you're all right," Christy says. She drops the tailgate and Cash leaps into the truck bed.

She wants the old me. I can handle this. I'm not crazy.

I slide into the backseat and Christy follows, putting her hand on mine. Joe drives off. I turn to look at the clinic as it shrinks in the rear window and squeeze Christy's hand tightly.

I'm never going back.

Chapter 18

The wildflowers in our yard are in full bloom; tall spikes of firecracker penstemon and short golden poppies surround a field of blue flax. The petals of the flax track the movements of the sun across the sky like small radar dishes. The big tooth maple tree next to the entry is lush with fresh growth. Green leaves flutter in the breeze and flap against the stout beams that hold up the shingle roof. The graceful eaves block out the summer heat, but allow the rays of the winter sun to flood the house with warmth. The grey stone slabs that hop scotch up to the front door are rugged and inviting.

It's exactly as I envisioned it on my drafting table four years ago. We'd maxed out our bank loan to get it finished. It was worth every penny. It's the best house in the neighborhood. I'm home now. I'm safe.

"It's nice to be home," I say, pushing open the front door with a black garbage bag draped over my back like a hobo at a homeless shelter. There's something about coming home that sets my mind at ease; the scent of lemon oil wafts off the furniture. Grids of luminescence spill across the floor from the mullions on the living room windows. My high school yearbook sits tattered and familiar between "Grapes of Wrath" and Frank Lloyd Wright's "Usonian Houses." Coconut infuses the air when I walk past the bathroom. It's Christy's favorite shampoo. It's where I belong, not in that Pine Sol clinic, at home with Christy. I can tell she's still nervous around me. She needs time to recover, to feel safe in our bed together. I'll wait for her to ask me.

"I'll share the guest bedroom with Joe," I say. I haul my clothes into the laundry room.

Christy is silent, an awkward affirmation of my new status. I'm no longer her reliable made-in-the-USA husband but a cheap import with a vacillating mental compass. I haven't been taking care of myself. I'm going to lose some weight, get back in shape, stop eating all that junk food and walk every day.

Joe and I stare at the double bed. "The last time we shared a bed we were stuck in the teardrop trailer with Mom," Joe says.

"I told you not to set up the tent so close to the stream."

"It was a freak flash flood."

"It was spring snowmelt."

"Left side or right?" I ask.

"Right," we say in unison.

"I'll flip you for it," I say. I pull out a quarter. "Heads, I win. Tails, you lose."

"You're a no good, lying cheat." he says. He shoves me across the room. We land on the bed. I slip from his grasp, roll and get Joe in a headlock. He kicks and flails his arms.

I watch his carotid artery collapse under my biceps.

He's turning pale, trying to say something. I summon every last ounce of strength to crush his windpipe. Christy runs into the room and screams, "No wrestling inside the house!"

"I get two points for the takedown," Joe says, gasping for breath.

"I scored two on the reversal," I say. I sit up and massage my back.

"I win on a near fall. Three points," I say.

"No way. Time expired."

"I had you pinned."

"I never tapped out."

Christy walks out of the room, mumbling about sibling rivalry.

"We're getting too old for this," Joe says. He pushes me off the bed.

"Tell me the truth." I sit down on the floor. "How's Mom?"

"She sleeps a lot, slipping in and out of consciousness."

She used to run me into the ground on her Sierra Club hikes. She had so much energy. "Is she in pain?"

"They started her on morphine. She doesn't have much time left. She asked me to let her behind the wheel, one last time," he says.

"You didn't let her on the freeway, did you?"

CHAPTER 19

I saved my money from stocking groceries at Trader Joes every summer and bought a used Mustang convertible my senior year of high school. Joe was busy most days with baseball practice, Daniel lived in a halfway house in Long Beach, and Richard Nixon was in the White House. Mom worked in downtown LA as a bookkeeper, commuting from Pasadena in rush hour traffic along the notorious Pasadena Freeway.

One of the first freeways built in California, it resembled a Grand Prix racetrack more than a highway. With five miles per hour off-ramps, no shoulders and a barrage of sharp S turns, this freeway was built for Model T's. Mom, however, relished this driver's derby. At the time, she drove the family station wagon-a Ford Country Squire with wood paneling on the exterior and a dual carb V-8 under the hood. When the transmission died, I offered to drive Mom to work in my Mustang till we saved enough money to get it fixed. She took me up under the condition she would drive.

Mom hopped behind the steering wheel at 7:30 a.m. I buckled up in the passenger seat.

"Better let the engine warm up for a few minutes," I said.

"We're running late," Mom said, zipping out into the traffic.

At the Arroyo Parkway entrance to the Pasadena Freeway, we hit a red light. With her hands clenched tight to the brown leather steering wheel, Mom sat watching precious seconds tick by, waiting for the light to turn green. When it did, my head snapped back from the sudden acceleration like a drag racer blasting off the starting line.

We slipped in front of a businessman in suit and tie driving a green Cadillac and hit the first S curve. I grabbed the handle on my door to resist the mounting G-forces that propelled the car towards the center divider.

Guard rail pickets flashed by the driver's side of the car just inches from the window as Mom dropped it into fourth gear. She was so focused on the road she failed to notice my clenched teeth. My shoulder slammed against the side door as the car banked into the second curve and the tires squealed. Accelerating through the curve, Mom caught up with the commuter traffic and dropped in twelve inches behind a Pontiac Firebird.

Traveling sixty miles per hour, surrounded by traffic only inches away, she passed cars at every chance. At the Santa Ana freeway off ramp, the traffic in the fast lane slowed to forty-five miles per hour while the exit-only lane sat empty. Seizing the moment, Mom swerved into the right lane and pushed the gas pedal to the floor. As we accelerated, the blood drained from my face.

"Why are we taking the exit?" I asked.

"Not to worry," she said, spotting a car length opening up in the lane ahead.

With the large metal lane divider directly in front of the car, Mom kept accelerating. I closed my eyes a second before impact. Suddenly Mom swerved hard left while simultaneously braking and slipped between two startled drivers in the fast lane.

"I passed ten cars with that move," she said, a smile beaming from her face.

"Nice," I said.

We pulled up to the curb at her downtown office building at 7:58, two minutes to spare. "Your little Ford has pretty good zip," she said, tossing me the keys.

Chapter 20

"No," Joe says. "I just let her drive around the empty parking lot at the hospice center."

"Erik, can you help me with dinner?" Christy calls out from the kitchen.

"I'll fire up the grille," I say, as I walk downstairs.

A crackling blaze sends flames that dance up the herringbone brick walls of the fireplace. The house smells of pine cones and cedar kindling. Cash hasn't spoken since we arrived home. He's sprawled out in front of the stone hearth like a sleepy lion. He casually lifts his head to see if his bowl has been filled and then slips back to his dreams.

Christy rolls the dough on the granite countertop for a pumpkin pie. Joe works on his laptop at the dining room table. I'm in charge of the tri-tip. I don't bake. I char.

I grab a nine-inch chef's knife off the rack to trim the fat off the steak. It's Damascus steel, hand forged in Japan like a samurai sword. The waves of alternating soft iron and high carbon steel form an intricate pattern that mimics the grain in a beautiful slab of burlwood.

You could really do some damage with this. That's an unsettling thought. I put the knife away; the fat can stay.

After a scrumptious meal, I clear the table. "I've got this," I say. I load the dishwasher. Christy nods approvingly.

Christy and Joe go through my discharge papers, therapeutic worksheets and medication spread across the coffee table.

"The list of Seroquel's side effects frightens me:" Christy says, "high blood pressure, thoughts of suicide, increased agitation, depression and loss of memory. There must be a safer, more holistic treatment."

"Your blood tests showed an extremely low vitamin D count," Joe says. "That can trigger depression."

"I'm on 5000 units of vitamin D," I say, taking another slice of pumpkin pie. I reach for the whip cream.

"Whoa there, Erik!" Joe says. "Drop the whip cream can very slowly and keep your hands visible."

"It's only my second," I say, waving the can in the air.

"**Third**," Joe and Christy say in unison. I set the can down. Nailed again.

Joe sifts through more handouts. "Exercise releases endorphins, dopamine, norepinephrine and serotonin," he reads. I'm so pale and pudgy. Christy and I used to go hiking every weekend. I miss that.

"Exercise is as effective as Prozac and psychotherapy for some depressed patients." Christy says, looking up from a pamphlet. Christy has always been into natural remedies. Those garlic pills she gave me when I caught pneumonia made me sweat garlic for a month, but they worked.

Minutes later, Christy and I share the couch with Cash at our feet. I put my arm around her. She snuggles in. It's nice to have her in my arms again.

"I'm myself," I say.

"You promised you'd follow Carson's advice," Christy says.

"I've got an appointment in the morning to meet with my new psychiatrist."

"Don't forget next week with Carson."

"It's on my day planner." She looks up at me.

"And the medication."

"Every morning and evening, like clockwork."

"You had a phone message last week from Mr. Anderson's secretary on the business line," she says. "He hired a different architect."

I've designed six lakefront estates. Now I can't even land a kitchen remodel. That guy was a jerk. I'm glad to be rid of him.

"I'll hustle up some work. It's just a road bump," I say.

"We could use the money right now," Christy says.

I need to hop back in the work saddle, and soon.

"I can't believe it's been over a year since I've had a job."

"Actually, it's been two years."

I'm losing track of time. Has it been that long? No wonder I got depressed. Work makes me feel useful. Oh, my God! I forgot to call Mom.

CHAPTER 21

I grab the phone and dial. "Hi Mom. It's me. How are you doing?"

"Erik?" The voice on the phone is faint and hesitant.

"I'm sorry I missed calling you last week."

"Joe said you were busy."

I was the man of the house after Daniel went into the hospital. I can't tell her she almost lost another son.

"Yeah, very busy, how are you doing?"

"I can barely raise my head off the pillow."

"I'll fly down in a few days. Maybe we can go out for dinner."

I want to tell her how much she means to me, but the words fail me.

"I haven't had much of an appetite lately, but it would be great to see you."

"I'll take you down to watch the women from your church group play bocce ball at the senior center."

"I'd like that," she says.

"Do you remember the time I took a poop in the plumbing display at the Sears store?" I say.

"You screamed, 'Mommy, there's no toilet paper' at the top of your lungs. I was mortified."

She laughs. It's a dulcet melody to my ears.

We talk for the next half hour. Her voice evaporates and reappears as we share memories of happier times: slivers from a lifetime of motherhood, nurturing three boys into men and sending us out into the world to discover our passions and strengths and frailties. She picked us off the pavement, wiped the blood from our shins and sent us back out with a whisper in our ear. "You can do it. You're my son." Joe and I hit our full strides. He as a lawyer, myself as an architect. Daniel stumbled and fell, but Mom never wavered in her support, even when he jumped off the freeway overpass and came home in a wheelchair. She drove him to therapy and helped him learn to walk with a cane. She braced him, encouraged him and celebrated his first steps once again. It was her role, her calling, her purpose. When Daniel died, so did a piece of her.

Now, after eighty-three years, all that is left on her plate are morsels of sweet memories and crumbs of regret. Nothing hearty to bite into, to nourish her dwindling appetite. She's worried about my knee. I'm worried about her cancer.

"Give Christy a hug for me," she says.

"You rest up."

Old age eats away at us: pecks at our eyes and nibbles on our heart. Our youthful vigor slips away and becomes nothing more than a wistful memory.

We arrive naked and scream for our first luscious gulp of air. In the end, we cling to each breath and beg for one more day to savor the world.

Chapter 22

The sun rises over the forest canopy, shooting beams of light through the bedroom window onto my pillow. I crawl out of bed and stand up. My back spasms. I collapse back onto the mattress. Joe rolls over and mumbles.

I ease myself onto the floor and shuffle towards the bathroom. Pills clutter the counter. I brush my teeth and stare at my meds: pain pills, sleeping pills, happy pills, vitamin pills, allergy pills. I've got a drug for every defect.

I spill my psych meds onto the counter. Guaranteed to cure melancholy and melt away ten pounds in one week or your money back! Side effects may include nausea and a euphoric sense of self-worth. If you experience an erection that lasts for more than four hours or a complete loss of all higher brain functions call Uber immediately for a ride to your nearest mortuary. If you are dissatisfied with your purchase for whatever reason, we promise a full refund, less shipping and handling fees. In addition, we will send you a complimentary set of ginsu steak knives at **no extra charge.**

I pull one pill from each bottle. Eye of newt, toe of frog, tongue of dog. I pop the pharmaceutical brew in my mouth. The gelatinous lump claws at my tongue as I swallow it whole.

I gag and vomit into my hand. It's a sewage pit of chemical salvation. I open my mouth and swallow again. The sludge slides down my gullet like a wriggling mass of sardines.

A surge of electricity shoots across my chest and down my legs. I topple to the floor. Sparks trickle from the hair on my arms. I lie there, numb and baffled, my heart races. I close my eyes. After a few minutes, I lift myself up and gaze at the mirror. My skin is blanched, a phantom crawling out of a casket. Maybe I had a heart attack. No. I've got a strong heart. It's the pills. They're going to kill me.

CHAPTER 23

The hallway to the doctor's office is stale and musty; the waiting room is half empty. The patients leave every other seat empty and avoid eye contact.

"I'm Erik Scott. I have an 8:30 appointment with Dr. Reed," I say to the receptionist when she slides the glass screen open.

"I'll need a photo ID and your insurance card," she says. She places a clipboard with forms on the counter in front of me. "Fill these out and we'll call you."

Forty-five minutes later, I'm led to a small examining room where I sit and wait another fifteen minutes, trying to stay awake.

"I'm Dr. Reed," the twenty-something in the white lab coat says, extending his hand.

His nails are meticulously manicured. We shake. "Erik Scott."

"I searched for your medical records, but we haven't received copies from the Behavioral Health Clinic yet."

I check his feet. He's wearing brown socks under his leather wing tips.

"Tell me about yourself. What were you treated for at the clinic?"

I tell him the condensed version of my anxiety, depression, and suicide attempt.

He scribbles on a pad of paper while I talk; he never acknowledges my pain or looks me in the eye or asks me a single question. I could be talking to an empty chair.

I am reminded of my first confession. Inside a black cubicle pouring out my sins to a faceless voice behind a wooden grille. The priest gave me a prescription for twenty Hail Marys and ten Our Fathers for finding Daniel's girlfriend so pretty I wondered what she looked like underneath her blouse.

The prayers did nothing to dissuade my pubescent infatuation with the opposite sex.

Finally, the rookie doc opens his mouth. "Was this your first suicide attempt?"

"First and last."

"What medication are you taking?"

"One hundred milligrams of Seroquel and twenty milligrams of Prozac."

"How's that working?"

"Good, so far."

"Well, you're bipolar. I'm going to switch you over to Lithium," he says. "You can stay on your current medication till the end of the month and then we'll make the transfer."

This guy made a snap diagnosis after a ten-minute meeting.

I stare at the floor for a minute, a dull ache in my chest. "How long will I stay on the Lithium?"

"The rest of your life," he says.

I can't chew cuckoo pills till the day I die. Look what they did to Daniel. He had an IQ over 140 and a photographic memory, but the pills left him in a stupor.

I stumble out the door with a prescription for a three-month supply of Lithium in my hand.

Chapter 24

I walk into the coffee shop. Joe flirts with the barista. She tosses back her hair with a flick of her hand. "Come back for a free refill, any time," she says. Joe drops five bucks in the tip jar.

She smiles.

"How'd it go?" he asks.

"He says I'm bipolar. Put me on Lithium, indefinitely."

"Daniel was bipolar; you're not."

Joe knows me better than anyone, except Christy.

"You're stubborn as a mule and obsessive compulsive," Joe says, "but no way bipolar."

"Is that your official diagnosis, Doctor?" I ask. "Erik Scott suffers from chronic mule brain syndrome?"

"I'm ordering a lobotomy and weekly treatment with a cattle prod."

Joe's right. That doctor's a quack.

• • •

The highway home climbs up from the desert plateau along the Truckee river. The sides of the canyon are pale brown, pierced with charred arrows, tree stumps stripped and lifeless, remnants of a wildfire. The blistered hills are littered with the cinders of mountain snowberry and gooseberry shrubs, twisted black tendrils scattered across the barren moonscape. On the river bank the first green saplings of cottonwood trees and sprouts of fireweed rise out of the ashes to begin rejuvenating the native landscape. I wonder how long it will take for the forest to recover.

"Doctors never fixed Daniel," I say.

"He never got the right treatment," Joe says, passing an eighteen-wheeler stacked with bales of hay.

"When he got out of Camarillo, he couldn't even remember how to play chess," I say. "I had to help him up the stairs to his bedroom."

Joe stares out the window. "I hate to think about him like that," he says. "I'd rather remember him for all the times he took me to the park to play catch."

The truck driver flashes his lights and Joe slips in front of the eighteen-wheeler.

"Remember when he'd throw us on his shoulders and race up and down the stairs?"

We pass a CHP parked on the side of the highway pointing a radar gun.

"It was the drugs," I said. "That's when he went berserk." A look of pain shoots across Joe's face. I stop talking.

We slow down for the Agricultural Inspection station. "I've got to quit these pills, before I end up like Daniel."

"Don't yoyo on and off your meds."

"I won't."

"Daniel would start to feel better, quit taking his medication to avoid the side effects, then spiral downward," Joe says.

"Where are you coming from?" the Ag. Officer asks.

"Reno," Joe says. He waves us through.

"Dr. Williams said some people leave the clinic and never need another pill."

"Don't you think that could be risky?"

"I'll be careful."

"What are you going to tell Christy?"

"I'll talk to her. I just need to find the right moment."

CHAPTER 25

Christy tends the garden out in the front yard as Joe drives us up to the house. She's wearing shorts and a sleeveless top. "Of all your beautiful curves, your smile is my favorite," I say.

"How is your new doctor?" Christy asks, looking concerned.

"I'm asking Carson for a second referral," I say.

"Why?"

"He said I was bipolar."

She shakes her head. "That doesn't make sense."

"Erik's not bipolar," Joe says.

"I'll find another MD," I say. "That kid didn't have any real-world experience."

"What about Carson?" Christy asks.

"He's just a therapist." I say. "He can't prescribe drugs. I'll get on the phone right away. I promise I'll get an appointment with another psychiatrist before the end of the month."

"You promise?" she says.

"Absolutely."

"I'll help," Christy says, setting down her spade. She follows us inside.

For three frustrating hours Christy, Joe and I work the phones. We make a list of all the psychiatrists in an eighty-mile radius. There are twenty-two. On the twentieth call, I get an appointment two months out, and I'll have to pay cash. They aren't in my insurance network. Finally, Christy calls Dr. Williams' office and gets another one-month prescription for my meds to bridge the gap.

I'll be better before then.

"You two take Cash out for some exercise," Christy says. "I'll pick up groceries for dinner."

CHAPTER 26

I lower the tailgate in the parking lot at Waterman's on Lake Tahoe and Cash bounds onto the asphalt. Joe throws two towels over his shoulder and locks up the truck.

"I'll go rent a two-man kayak," Joe says. "Take Cash for a walk."

Cash and I trek down the beach to a secluded spit of sand that juts out into the cerulean waters. Cash drops his head on my lap. We bask in the bright sunshine.

I rub the short black hair on the crown of Cash's head. Small waves lap at the sand surrounding us, the lake exhales softly with each successive ebb and flow.

I wish I had somebody to talk to.

"Talk to me," Cash says.

My hands recoil off his fur. "Dogs can't talk."

"We both know that," Cash says. "Remember what your Mom said?"

"Normal is just a setting on the clothes dryer," I say, "but this is weird."

"Why don't you talk to Joe?" The wave dissolves into the sand.

"I can't tell him I'm hallucinating."

"Why not?" A father leads his infant son to the water's edge, a stone's throw down the beach.

"We lived through that with Daniel."

"How about Carson?"

"I'll get locked up." The brown-haired boy, his arching belly sticking out of a red sun top, drops his father's hand and runs into the lake.

"Christy?" Cash asks.

"She's too fragile."

"If you don't share this with her, it will drive you apart."

"I can't dump this on her right now." The boy stops and stares. The cold water swirls around his chubby white feet.

I scratch Cash's lower back. His rear leg twitches and he rolls onto his side. "That leaves me then," he says.

"I'm all fucked up inside," I say.

"What makes you say that?"

"I hurt so much that I'm losing hope."

"Hope for what?" he asks.

"That I'll ever feel good again."

"But you've got Christy and Joe," he says.

"I don't want to drag them down with me."

"But they love you."

I hear Joe call me from down the beach. I smile meekly at the man and his son as Cash and I walk back along the shore. The little boy waves at me.

I'm losing my sanity. I can't let anyone know I'm talking to my dog.

• • •

"Put on this vest and slide in the front seat," Joe says, holding the kayak steady. I plop my butt unceremoniously into the fiberglass shell and clip the snaps on the life preserver. Joe hands me a paddle and jumps into the rear seat, while he pushes us off. The kayak tips side to side, leaving me shaky. Is this what it feels like when sailors abandon ship?

Cash sits in the hull of the boat at my feet and looks over the bow of the kayak. I stroke awkwardly as we paddle into the lake. "Left, right, left, right," Joe says. My movements smooth out and our blades dip in unison, slicing through the crystal-clear water. It's a blue-sky day, the kind that remind me why I moved here. Freel Peak wears a cap of snow that lingers on its north face till the summer sun rises in the sky to transform winter squalls into life nourishing water for the forest below. The lake is calm, a sheet of glass that allows me to admire the granite slabs scattered across the bottom of the lake twenty feet below us. A school of minnows darts away from the shadow of our boat. Cash barks at them.

"What ever happened to Stacy?" I ask. "You two were a good match."

"She met someone else."

"Are you ever going to settle down with anyone?"

"I'm not cut out to be married, or a father for that matter," Joe says.

My paddle skips out of the water and hits Joe's blade.

"Why do you say that?" I say. "You'd be a great dad."

"I don't have the patience to raise a kid."

Left. Right. Left. Right. We're back in sync.

"We didn't have much of a paternal role model growing up, did we?"

"We were lucky to be younger than Daniel," Joe says.

Daniel spent a lot of time locked in his bedroom alone. Dad didn't know how to talk to him.

Joe dips his blade behind the kayak to turn us back towards the shore. My paddle gets heavier by the minute.

"Dad did the best he could," I say. Mom told us his father used to beat him.

I'm going to start exercising regularly.

He never hit us, except that time I borrowed our neighbor's bike without asking. I deserved that. Maybe I'll buy a kayak.

Boy am I out of shape.

CHAPTER 27

Christy and I wade through the mound of mail scattered across the kitchen table, while Joe takes a shower. "Here's the gas bill," I say, putting it in the stack for Christy. "Important notice" is stamped in red on the next envelope. It's an overnight special delivery.

I rip it open and read, "My health insurance company says I'm close to maxing out my mental health benefits." I grind my teeth.

"What are you talking about? You just got out of the hospital."

"My policy has a limit of $20,000 for behavioral health treatments and the emergency room bill along with the anticipated bill from my seventy-two hour hold in the clinic will probably exceed the limits of my coverage." My head starts to throb.

"I'll call the insurance company," Christy says. She runs upstairs to the office and I muddle through the remaining mail, unaware of what I'm reading. She comes downstairs, shaking her head.

"We may owe a few thousand dollars. They won't know the final costs for several weeks." Christy rubs the back of her neck.

I drop my face into my hands and sigh. "This is going to put a big hole in our saving," I say.

Christy and I sit, sullen, in the kitchen. "What's the matter?" Joe asks, drying his hair with a towel.

"I maxed out my health insurance," I say. "We may owe them money."

"How much?" Joe asks.

"We'll have to tap into our emergency savings."

"Let me know if I can help," Joe says. "I have a rainy-day account with a few thousand in it."

"Thanks, Joe," I say. "We'll be fine."

Chapter 28

Joe and Christy go for a walk into the woods, leaving me with Cash on the back patio.

"I blew it," I say, "by landing in a loony bin."

"Don't blame yourself," Cash says as they disappear into the forest.

"Who else am I supposed to blame?"

"If you beat yourself up, you're going to feel worse."

"If I'm not hard on myself, I'll turn soft," I say.

"Everything happens for a reason," Cash says.

"What possible good could come from this?" I ask. "I tried to off myself, hurt Christy, got stuck in a nuthouse and now I owe money for the whole mess!"

"Maybe there's a lesson here."

"What's the lesson?"

"I'm not Siri," Cash says. "That's for you to figure out."

"Give me a hint at least."

"Why don't you give Christy a bouquet of flowers?" Cash says.

"That's a great idea."

"Let's walk down to the market."

"I'll buy her a dozen red roses and write her an apology."

"And buy her some fresh bones."

A half hour later, I arrange the flowers in Christy's favorite vase. Cash gnaws on a bone. Where are they? I empty the dishwasher and mop up the kitchen floor.

• • •

It's been over an hour. The roses are drooping. What's taking them so long?

Joe and Christy walk in the front door.

I give Christy the vase. "This is for you, honey," I say, "I also had a bone for you," handing her the empty butcher's paper, "but Cash got to it first."

Cash walks up and drops his half-eaten bone at her feet.

She laughs. It's her first laugh in weeks.

"I'll leave you two alone," Joe says. "I'll call Mom."

"I'm sorry I lost the Anderson job," I say.

"I'll talk to my shift supervisor about getting some extra hours at the hospital," she says. She shouldn't need to do that.

"I've been making your life miserable." This is all my fault.

"You need to rest and recharge for a few days."

This has been a lousy week.

"Let's get a massage together, I say." Christy loves that girly stuff.

"That's sweet, but we can't afford that right now."

Just then, Joe walks back into the room.

"Mom hasn't eaten in two days," he says.

"Is she awake?" I ask.

This could be it. I have to hold myself together. She needs me.

"I'll fly down to check on Mom," Joe says.

"I'll go with you," I say.

"You should stay here," Joe says.

He's right. I need to fix things with Christy.

Joe looks over as Christy.

"Go," she says, "we'll be fine."

CHAPTER 29

Christy and I had been married for six years and bought our first house, an old log cabin on the west shore of Lake Tahoe for forty-five thousand dollars. It was a fortune. I was glued to the TV watching the first pictures from a catastrophic nuclear disaster in Chernobyl, Ukraine. The phone rang.

"Hello, this is officer Rex Beck of the Burney, Idaho police department. Are you related to a Harriet Scott?"

"Yes, she's my mother."

"Well, Mr. Scott, we've got your mother in custody here in Burney, Idaho for resisting arrest. She was cited for driving sixty miles per hour in a forty-mile zone. When I pulled her over, she seemed disoriented and confused. I asked her to step out of the car. She was belligerent and told me she was in a hurry. It took me five minutes to talk her out of the car. That's when I noticed she wasn't wearing any shoes. While I ran her license plate, she jumped back in the driver's seat and drove off. I had to chase her down in my patrol car. I was forced to bring her into the police station in handcuffs. I apologize for the handcuffs, but your mother would not cooperate."

Knowing how bullheaded my mom could be, I was beginning to feel sorry for "Officer Rex Beck." I could just see this big burly policeman haul my sixty-year-old mom, punching and yelling, into the police station in handcuffs while his fellow officers watched in amusement.

I broke out laughing, "This is a great story, Joe, you've really outdone yourself."

"I assure you, Mr. Scott, this is no joke. Your mother, Mrs. Harriet Scott, is in custody for resisting arrest and as a courtesy I've called you."

"Oh shit," I said. "I thought this was a prank call. Is my mom OK?"

"She looks tired and slightly disoriented but refused a physical. She shouldn't be driving. I don't want her in lockup. If you come pick her up, I'm willing to take her to the Best Western."

I thought for a second.

"I can be in Idaho tomorrow afternoon. Can I speak to my mom?"

I hear footsteps on the other end of the line.

"Erik?"

"Mom, are you OK?"

"I'm fine, but I have to get to New York. Myrtle is in the hospital."

"What for?"

"They don't know. She just collapsed."

"Officer Beck says you look tired and confused. He wants me to come pick you up."

"Don't worry, son. I'm OK."

"He said you resisted arrest. If I don't go there, he'll put you in lockup."

"I can't spend the night in jail. I need to go see Myrtle."

"Why don't you fly?"

"Those contraptions aren't safe. I'm driving."

"Officer Beck has agreed to set you up in a motel for tonight. I'll fly to Idaho in the morning. We can drive to New York together."

"You don't need to fly out here. It's a waste of time and money."

"If I pay will you stay at the Best Western tonight? Tomorrow night we can go out for a nice dinner and then both leave for New York the next morning. OK?"

There was a long pause at the other end of the line. "Well, all right," she said.

Officer Beck came back on the line. "Mr. Scott, what did you decide?"

"I'll be there tomorrow," I said.

The next day, I packed my bags and drove to the airport at noon. I felt like a Canadian Mountie heading out to rescue the damsel in distress.

I stepped out of my rental car at the Best Western Inn in Burney, Idaho at 5:51 p.m. My back was killing me. I walked up to the front desk. A lean bald man with a handlebar mustache watched TV behind the counter.

"Can you tell me what room Mrs. Harriet Scott is in?"

"Mrs. Scott checked out this morning," he said, without taking his eyes off the TV.

"What?"

"You must be Erik. Your mother left this note," he said:

> Erik,
>
> I tried to call you at home. No answer. I spoke with my sister late last night. She has cancer. I couldn't wait. I knew you would understand.
>
> Love,
> Mom

I jumped in my rental car and headed back to the airport. Joe and I shared a good laugh when I told him the story.

Mom called me at home two days later. She'd made the two-thousand-three-hundred-mile drive from Burney Idaho to Staten Island, New York in fifty hours. She drove the whole way in bare feet.

Chapter 30

Christy and I watch Joe drive off to the airport. Mom will be fine once Joe arrives. I wipe off Cash's paws in the entry while Christy goes to take a shower. A blood curdling scream fills the house. Christy comes running, "There's something in my bed!"

I race to the master bedroom. Between the sheets lies the rigid corpse of a squirrel. Its eyes are vacant orbs of glass.

"Gross," I say.

"Get that creature out of my bed!" Christy says.

"I'll get some gloves from the shed."

After I put the cadaver in a paper bag, I strip the bed. Christy paces the hall, her arms tightly wrapped around her chest.

"How did it get into my bed?" she says.

"It probably crawled in looking for a warm place to die, that or Cash was sharing his latest hunting trophy with you."

"Not mine," Cash barks. I give him a dirty look.

"You'd better give Cash a bath with flea powder," I say, "in case the squirrel is infected with the plague."

"Wait a second," says Cash.

I feel dizzy.

"I'll take Cash," Christy says. "We both need a shower." She drags Cash off. He tugs against her all the way into the bathroom.

I walk out of the house and hold the critter in the paper bag with outstretched hands, like a sacrificial offering in a pagan ritual. The moon casts shapeless forms across the forest floor. A bat flits past, chasing some hapless insect. I dig a small hole where a shaft of light strikes the barren dirt. I pull the squirrel from the bag and hold it in the moon's glow.

"Alas poor squirrel, I knew ye not. You look old. White flecks of hair speckle your mottled face. Did old age cripple you so? We are both creatures of flesh and blood. Did you grow too old to forage for food, too senile to attract a mate, too weak to fend off the disease that ravaged your mind and set you on a search for your final resting spot? Did you live an honorable life? Did you keep your wife warm during winters cold embrace? How do you measure the worth of a squirrel? Did you keep her safe and filled with mirth? Where are your gibes and gambols now? When the last spark of life went dark were you at peace? What did you do to deserve such an unsightly demise? In our final days, we wonder at our worth. A pile of dust or a life brimming with succulent morsels rich with flavor? Will I leave life's table satiated or angry, screaming at my empty bowl or licking my lips? Will I lose my appetite for life or savor every delicious moment? We must all face the inevitable. We are all born from a mother's womb. We will all wither to dust. It is what we do in between that makes us unique.

I slip the squirrel in the bag. I gently lay him in the ground. I sprinkle him with dust.

• • •

Christy and I lie under a blanket on the couch later that evening. I've got an ice pack on my lower back as she rubs my shoulders. "Is your back any better?"

"It is now."

She smells inviting. The fire crackles and Cash dozes at our feet.

I kiss her gently on her head. She pulls me closer. "I think I pulled a muscle in my right hamstring."

Her hands move down my back and reach around my waist to gently massage my right thigh.

"Is that better?"

"You're a miracle worker. All my aches and pains are gone."

I reach under the blanket and wrap my arm around her waist. She puts her hand on mine and pats it. It's her way of saying not tonight, dear.

How long it will take to win her back?

CHAPTER 31

After kissing Christy goodnight, I brush my teeth and pull my psych meds from the cabinet. The longer I take these pills, the more they will decimate my brain. I don't need this pharmaceutical crutch.

I've run my own architectural business for years.

I'm a success.

I've been married for over thirty years.

I have the willpower to do this.

I've never been to a shrink. Never needed one. I'm healthy. This was a onetime problem. I'm ready to put this behind me. Get back to my old self. I believe in myself.

I open the bottles and dump all the pills into the sink and watch the whirlpool suck the swirling mass of pills down the drain. I scrape the last few pills out of the sink before they disappear into the sewer. I watch them dissolve into a slimy white paste on my fingertips. My confidence disintegrates with them.

I should have kept a few pills for emergencies.

• • •

It's one AM. I'm wide awake. I kick the covers off my sweaty limbs. The demons thrive in the dark. They come at me in waves. The bed heaves and I'm tossed by the current and carried out to sea in the darkness. I struggle to keep my head above water as the waves pitch me about. I see the first massive wall of fear mongering water curl over me. It crashes and floods my nose with bitter brine. The water pounds in my ears. You're broken. You don't deserve her.

I'm trapped underwater with the voices of despair till my lungs are ready to burst. I breach the surface, gasping for air. Another giant cliff of whitewater rolls towards me. I take a desperate gulp of air and dive. I tumble like a rag doll in the violent churning froth of hopeless misery. She doesn't love you. You're crazy.

Another wave crashes over me. My lungs scream. I've got to get to the surface. I leap from the bed dripping with sweat. I won't make it through the night.

CHAPTER 32

I lumber downstairs to find pliers and a tea strainer. I lay on my back under the vanity and unhook the drain trap. I slowly pour the sludge from the trap into the strainer over the toilet. A slimy white hairball forms in the bottom of the mesh. My last chance for medical salvation is a hairball.

I can't do it. I flush it down the toilet.

It's three AM.

The nights are the worst. I have no one to distract me from my demented apprehensions. I crawl out of bed and sneak down to the office. I'll look at the bookkeeping. I've been afraid to look at our account balances ever since I ran out of work. The check book registers are out of balance. I dig through the files to find our monthly bank statements. They don't make sense. There's only two hundred dollars in our emergency fund!

We had thirty grand.

We're heading toward bankruptcy! We'll be homeless. Everything I've worked for. Gone. Christy's been hiding this.

I storm down stairs and barge into the master bedroom. Cash looks up from the foot of the bed. "Quiet, you'll wake her."

"She and I need to talk."

The bedcovers rustle.

"Let's go for a walk," Cash says, "outside." He jumps up and springs past me.

The moon plays hide and seek behind drab grey clouds that march across the sky like soldiers returning from battle: muddied and bloodied and asleep on their feet. The tall spires of sugar pine trees are visible above the forest canopy; sentinels to protect the walking wounded who trudge through the trenches. The long cylindrical cones on the uppermost boughs glisten with ice, sending prisms of light down to the pine needle carpet like wispy lanterns that swing with the breeze. The wind whispers a melancholy tune that blankets the forest with apprehension.

"What are you doing?" Cash asks. "It's the middle of the night."

"We're going broke. It's Christy's fault."

"Don't blame her. She's working extra shifts."

"She didn't tell me we were running out of money."

"You were in no shape to hear it."

"I deserved to know."

"She was trying to avoid the stress it would cause you."

"I can handle it."

Cash and I argue back and forth for what seems like hours.

"I'm exhausted," I finally say. A band of light pierces through the clouds that stumble off the edge of the horizon on the eastern front.

"Go get some sleep," Cash says.

Chapter 33

I turn over and hug my pillow. The clock on the nightstand says 7:00 AM. I lumber out of bed and open the blinds. The morning sun melts the icy crystals that encapsulate the sugar cones, luminescent beads of water tumble to the lower branches. The rhythmic splash sounds like a metronome. Drip. Drip. Drip. Two white downy goshawk chicks are startled awake by the dew drops splattering on their oversize nest. Drip. Drip. Drip. They squawk "ke ke ke" for their mother who takes flight as the first rays of the sun breach the forest canopy and soars high above the tree tops, hunting for their next meal.

"Blueberry pancakes in ten minutes," I hear from downstairs.

"I'm up."

I need to talk to Christy.

I shuffle off to the bathroom. I'm shaky. I brush my teeth and notice water dripping on my feet.

I thought it was a bad dream.

I towel off the water and put the p-trap back. Nobody needs to know.

"I went over our bank statements last night after you went to bed," I say.

Christy stops stirring the batter. She sets the wooden spoon on the counter.

I stand in front of her. "Why didn't you tell me?"

"We've been hemorrhaging money for several months." She steps back.

"You should have told me sooner."

Her gaze drops to the floor. "I thought I could make it up."

"We may have to declare bankruptcy."

She places her hands around my neck. "We'll get through this." She massages my rigid shoulders.

We sit quietly, eating pancakes. My insides bubble with caustic chemicals that burn a hole through my stomach lining. I should have never lost that Anderson job.

She pours some coffee in my cup. "You should call Joe, see how your mom is doing."

She's looking out for me.

Joe has good news. Mom perked up when he arrived. She ate a bagel with cream cheese. I promise I'll fly down. Soon.

As I hang up, the phone rings.

"Erik, It's Robert." He's my favorite contractor. "The Sullivan house is flooded. Six inches of standing water everywhere."

The news chomps another hole in my gut.

"What happened?"

"Remember the steam unit Mrs. Sullivan had us add in the master shower."

"Sure, I had you install it in the attic."

"It froze and burst. The cleaning lady found the mess."

"How bad is it?"

"All the hardwood flooring and carpets are ruined. Cabinets are warped. We're tearing the sheetrock off the walls two feet up. It's going to cost several hundred thousand dollars."

"Their homeowner's insurance will cover it."

"They're suing us."

"What?"

"You'd better lawyer up. I'm sorry to be the bearer of bad news," Robert says. He hangs up.

I rummage through the files in my office for the next two hours. I forgot to draw insulation in the rafters over the steam unit on the change order. Robert should have caught that. The lawyer fees alone will wipe me out, not to mention a huge settlement. At least, they can't take the house.

"How's your Mom?" Christy asks.

"She got her appetite back."

"That's good. She's still fighting back."

"I'm taking Cash out for a walk," I say. I clip him to his leash and head out the front door.

We walk deep into the woods, where bark beetles have decimated the drought stricken lodgepole pines that litter the winding dirt pathway, worm riddled skeletons mowed down by violent storms.

"You should tell her," Cash says.

"She didn't tell me our savings were gone."

"She was paying the bills."

"You knew you were eating through your savings. You didn't want to face it."

We walk for the next hour in utter silence while the gorilla grunts and gibbers and screeches deep inside my head. As we walk back down the driveway, a van pulls in behind me.

"Mr. Erik Scott?" the driver asks.

"That's me."

He hands me a clipboard. "Sign here."

I scribble my name. He gives me a letter and drives off.

It's from our bank. It's a notice of default. They're foreclosing on our house in ninety days.

CHAPTER 34

Entering through the side door of the kitchen, I hear Christy on the phone. "I'll call you back."

She's hiding things from me.

"Who was that?" I ask.

"Joe."

I fold my arms across my chest. "Are you two talking behind my back?"

"We're concerned."

"You're concerned about me?"

She hangs up the phone. "Of course."

"But not enough to tell me you haven't paid the mortgage."

She runs her fingers through her hair. "We'll make it up."

"I'll remember that when we're homeless."

"We're just a little behind," she says.

I throw the paperwork at her feet. "They're taking our house. The bank filed for foreclosure."

Christy's face turns pale. "Joe will help us out. I can start to work double shifts at the hospital."

"We're going to be out on the street!" I stand over her as she kneels down to collect the papers scattered across the floor. Her hands shake.

"You've been spending money like there's no tomorrow!"

"That's because I didn't know we were almost broke."

She stands up. "You knew." She pokes my chest. "You kept playing golf with your buddies."

"Don't blame this on me!"

"You haven't worked in two years."

I step back. "Cash could do a better job running this household!" I say. I turn. "Right, Cash?"

Cash is silent.

"Look at yourself, Erik. You're talking to the dog."

"He's got more sense than you."

She scowls at me. "You're the liar! I heard you on the phone. The Sullivans are suing us."

I set my hands on my hips. "At least they couldn't take our house. My business is incorporated. But you took care of that. You let the bank have the house."

"It's only four walls and a roof."

"It's everything I've worked for." I yank the flowers out of the vase and throw them at Christy's feet. "Get out of my house!"

• • •

I hear Christy drive out of the garage. Cumulonimbus clouds billow across the sky. Only thin slivers of light slip through cracks in the blustering firmament. The clap of thunder roars in the distance.

She's left me. It's over.

A field mouse scurries back to his underground burrow. Trumpets of rain sound from the sky. What have I done?

The sky unleashes a torrent of fury so unrelenting that the stalks of camas lilies are toppled to the ground and their delicate blue petals are awash in the mire. She's the love of my life. I have to get her back.

Afternoon thundershowers pound the waters of Lake Tahoe. I run downstairs and race down the driveway. Droplets bounce off the surface so thick and so fast it forms a tapestry of turbulence that makes water and air indistinguishable. I pant and double up before I reach the street. She's gone.

I walk back to the safety of my house. The one I've scraped and saved for. The one I'm about to lose, along with my wife.

Chapter 35

The phone rings constantly, but I don't care. How could this happen to me? As night descends the demons slip from cracks in the walls to whisper sweet lies. I need to talk to Cash. He'll help me figure this out.

I stagger down the hallway. I haven't slept for God knows how long. I trip over dirty dishes and eat the leftover sandwiches I find on the floor. I hear buzzing, buzzing, buzzing in my head.

"Go away!" I scream.

"It's me, honey. It's Christy."

There's a rush of cold air. Christy's face is inches away.

"You look exhausted. Cash and I were worried. You didn't answer the phone." I hear a loud bark. A cold nose brushes my hand. Cash came back to me!

"I want to take you back to the clinic."

Something lands on my shoulder. I shove it away.

"Don't touch me!" Her face retreats into the woodwork.

"I don't want to lose you. I worked out a payment plan to cover your treatment."

"We'll be penniless!"

Christy's face emerges from the refrigerator door. "You're more important than money."

"I can't go back. They'll lobotomize me. Turn me into a drooling imbecile."

"You're going to hurt yourself."

"What do you think, Cash?" He'll know what to do.

"You should listen to her." I turn, but he's nowhere.

"You two are bullying me," I say. "I can do this on my own."

My teeth gnash and grind.

"Look at yourself, Erik. You're asking Cash for medical advice."

"He's my best buddy." The room spins.

"If you don't go voluntarily, I'll have you committed." My chest collapses; reason drains out the floodgates at my feet, spilling my sanity across the floor. Cash barks.

"You can't. I haven't done anything."

"I'll call the police and tell them you assaulted me."

The rabid gorilla shreds the inside of my brain with his razor-sharp teeth, circling and attacking. I scream and yell but he keeps ripping the nerves out of my tortured skull. I am helpless to stop him.

"That's a lie. Don't do this." My chest implodes, my legs crumble like the walls of a collapsing dam. The floor starts to swallow me.

"I'll do whatever it takes to save you. I'm calling the police."

Daniel told me what they did. I won't let that happen to me.

"Send the police. My husband is trying to assault me. Hurry!"

"She's lying!" The floorboards lock around my feet. I can't reach the phone to rip it from the wall.

"Send the police immediately. He's violent."

For five minutes, my head builds pressure. Water boils and steam rises off the surface of my seething anger. My bubbling cauldron is about to erupt and spew columns of molten rage across the room. I hear the sirens in the distance.

"Help is coming, honey. Hang on a little longer."

I know better. Only I can fix this. If I go back to the clinic my skeleton will be piled on the rocky shoals of Greece with all the other fools seduced by the sounds of Homer's Sirens. I'll finish this. Right here. Right now.

No. I can't hurt Christy. Never again.

"I'm sorry."

"Are you OK? They're here, honey. They've come to take you to the hospital."

A flotilla of blue masses down the hall. Who do they think they are? This is my house.

"Stay back!"

"Please put down that knife, Erik. The police have guns."

Molten rage spews from my heart and descends into a cold, deep pool of shame. I can't live like this anymore. This is my only way out.

"Stay away, Ma'am."

"Erik. Don't do this! Let them take you to the hospital."

"I'd rather die." I see blood spurt out of my hand. I feel nothing.

"Drop the weapon, sir, or we'll shoot."

"Fire away. I'm as good as dead!"

"Oh my God! Don't shoot him. He needs help." It's Christy's voice, a pool of tranquility inside the savage tempest that rips my sanity from its mooring.

She loves me.

Christy squeezes me with all her might when suddenly she's swept aside and I swing and push and thrash against a sea of blue uniforms that bury me like a wave breaking over a crash test dummy. My hairless mannequin arms are twisted and bent and cuffed behind my back and I'm dragged down the hall flopping my lower torso like a fish impaled on a gaff, my eyes bulging, my gills desperately flapping for one last gasp of oxygen and I scream.

"Please don't put me away. I'll die in there!"

Part Three

"But I don't want to be with mad people," Alice said.
"Oh, you can't help that, said the Cat, "we're all mad here.
I'm mad. You're mad." "How do you know I'm mad?"
Alice asked.
You must be," said the Cat, "or you wouldn't be here."[4]

CHAPTER 36

I'm being dragged into the clinic like a side of beef, hanging on a hook, sliding down a stainless-steel track in the slaughterhouse. Eli is under my left arm. Maru is under my right. I should be kicking and screaming and howling like a rabid dog, but I can't. I'm just a slab of meat.

My wife committed me.

My body is falling apart.

My business is in shambles.

My house is gone.

I'm broke.

Maybe this is where I'm supposed to be.

Nurse Lisa holds a fresh pair of blue hospital scrubs, a shower head and a pair of white flip flops in her hands. I stand in silence and stare at her for a long minute.

"You've been in the county hospital under sedation for three days, Erik. Now you're back with us. You know the rules. You need to take a shower and put on clean clothes as part of the admittance process."

That's why I feel so groggy. I try to pull my right arm out from Maru's viselike grip. I'm not going anywhere.

I'm just like Larry.

I take the scrubs and meekly walk down the hall accompanied by my henchmen.

"Are you going to be OK?" Maru asks.

I nod. The stitches on the palm of my right-hand throb and my head pulses. It expands and contracts like a bloated watermelon rotting on the vine in the scorching summer sun, ready to explode and spew bright red spongy fruit onto the ceiling and across the room at Charles's feet.

"You're back," he says, standing in the open doorway. "Don't hog the hot water."

"I missed the food," I say.

• • •

Half an hour later, I lie on the bed as Charles walks in from the bathroom, toweling off his lean, sinewy frame. His hands are knobby and bark encrusted, roughhewn from years of manual labor.

"What happened?" Charles asks.

"Christy had me committed."

He wipes off the beads of water that glisten on his brown suede shoulders. A black obsidian arrowhead rests on his breastbone, dangling from a leather necklace.

"Why?"

"I'm hallucinating."

"We call it Hanbleceyapi."

"What's that?"

"A vision quest."

"It's more like a nightmare."

Charles sits down across from me. The skin on his legs is scarred and cracked, like a catcher's mitt worn out from too many seasons of blocking fast balls in the dirt. "Tell me what's going on," he says.

"I've been having conversations with my dog, Cash."

"Is he black or white?"

"He's black."

He nods his clean-shaven head.

I sit up. "No, he's not like that."

"They're never simple." Charles's feet are broad and scaly, the color of a mud.

"I doubt anyone could make sense of what I'm going through, least of all me."

"Give yourself time to understand the meaning. It's not easy."

"It's not a vision."

"If you say so," he says.

I admire Charles. He sees the world through the filter of his spiritual beliefs. Not religious, per se, the universe as one cohesive orb of planets and people, plants and animals, soil and water; everything flows to the rhythm of a single spirit who oversees the scenes unfolding below.

I see it much different, cold and heartless, chaotic and confusing, driven by fierce competition and survival of the fittest; each person strives to get ahead and make a good life, despite the odds. I thought I controlled my own destiny. Maybe I'm wrong. Maybe I do need help.

• • •

"Erik, how are you?" Dr. Williams asks, gently rubbing my shoulder. He grabs the desk chair and pulls it up in front of me, ready for the interrogation.

"I'll give you two some privacy," Charles says. He steps into tattered work pants and a tee shirt and ambles out the door.

Dr. Williams looks up from the chart in his hand.

"What do you and your dog talk about?"

"Christy, most of the time."

"Does he tell you to do violent things?"

He's got a tough job. He's got thirty minutes per patient to plug the gaping holes in our psyche with little round pills and a few choice words, slobber on a spitball.

"Of course not." He scribbles some notes.

"Is he a voice or a thought inside your head?"

"I'd say both."

"Have you been taking your medication?"

"I stopped cold turkey a few days ago. The Seroquel gave me a heart attack."

The spittle makes the pill expand. But it's an art. You have to get the right pill for the shape of the hole. You need the correct amount of dribble and great timing.

"Exactly what happened?"

"I swallowed a pill and the next thing I knew a bolt of electricity arched across my chest, my heart starting racing and I felt faint. Then the hair on my arms stood up and my hands tingled."

"How long did it last?"

"I'd guess ten minutes."

"And how long between the time you took the pills and the attack?"

"Only a matter of seconds."

"The medication would take several minutes to absorb into your bloodstream, not seconds. You had a panic attack, not a heart attack."

A good psychiatrist needs fresh saliva, not that old school Freudian drool. Pills and science, therapeutic spit wads designed to plug the cracks in my psyche. Like I said. It's an art form. Maybe this guy is Picasso.

"Have you been sleeping?"

"I don't know. The bank is foreclosing on my house."

"I'm sorry to hear that," Dr. Williams says.

"We'll start you back on the Prozac. It will help with the stress."

Maybe he's not Picasso, more like Thomas Kincaid. Good with a brush. Nice technique. Master of light on dark canvases. Definitely prolific. There's big turnover at this gallery.

"Will these hallucinations go away?"

"I've had good results with Seroquel, just be patient."

"I've got nothing but time, Doc."

"I may adjust dosages or switch medication, but we'll get it figured out."

"How long will this take?"

"It could be weeks or months. If you hallucinate, just stay calm and recognize it's not real."

"What if I can't tell the difference?"

"You're more cognizant than most of my patients. Write down what you experience and talk to me. We'll get you back on your own two feet."[5]

"That's good to hear, Doc. Thanks."

He taps me on the knee and walks out the door. He's wearing Birkenstock sandals. I've got a flower child for shrink, a Picasso with flip flops.

Chapter 37

I walk into the recreation room and survey the damaged goods scattered across the room. Within seconds, I'm surrounded by the welcoming committee.

"Look who's back in the nuthouse!" Alex shouts. His wispy beard is interrupted by patches of pallid rind and his hand flickers, evidence his moonshine scurvy still rages.

"Hey there, stranger," Gina says. She coils the snake on her arm under my shoulder and leads me to the couch. "Did you miss us?" she asks. I didn't realize she was so striking. She reminds me of a young Christy, but a brunette.

"I couldn't stay away."

"You're on track to break Charles's record of four times back in the clinic, if you keep up this pace," Alex says.

"That's not a record I want to own."

"Records are made to be broken," Charles says.

Sandy's still wearing her pink pajamas. They must be glued to her skin.

"What did you do to your hand?" she asks.

My heart surges to five thousand rpm's and sweat bubbles out of my radiator cap. I can't tell them I sliced open my own hand.

"I slipped and cut my hand with a kitchen knife."

"You're lucky you didn't cut any ligaments," Gina says.

I'm grilled for the next ten minutes, but I don't mind. They don't chastise me for my weakness of mind and poor judgement. We're all rejects here, with some chip or blemish or flaw in manufacturing that sends us back to the returns department to be reconditioned and repainted and repackaged.

• • •

It's exercise hour. I head outside the clinic with Mary, one of the counselors and a group of patients for an afternoon walk in the park across the street. Eli stands at the security door and checks our names on his clipboard. An asphalt path circles an expanse of fresh cut lawn in the center of the park. At the far end of the grass two cottonwood trees stand, a concrete table and bench sits in the shade beneath their canopy. The group circles the park and disperses into smaller groups as the slower walkers drop off the pace. The heat of the asphalt rises up through my flip flops, warming my toes. There is a slight breeze that brings small tufts of white cotton drifting down from the tree tops. Alex walks beside me, reading a crumpled sheet of paper. He lights a cigarette. His hand shakes.

"Those things are going to kill you," I say. I glance over his shoulder. It's "The Twelve Steps."

"The booze will finish me off before that."

I love Alex's bleak humor.

"How's your rehab going?"

"I'm fucked." The scurvy's spread to his tongue.

"Why?"

"I'm an atheist, so taking a searching and fearless moral inventory of myself is a real bitch."

"It's hard to look yourself in the mirror."

"It's not a pretty picture," Alex says. "I'm a mean drunk. How do I make it up to my daughter for all the soccer games

I missed? I can't take back all the crap I screamed at my wife."

"I did something terrible to Christy."

His head droops. "I'll never make it through twelve steps."

"Let me see." He hands me the list. We continue to walk. I just admitted to another person the exact nature of my wrongs. That's step five.

"It's simple in theory, but hard as hell in practice," Alex says.

As we approach the end of the park, Alex plunks down on the concrete bench. His t-shirt is drenched in sweat. The woodsy scent from the cottonwood trees masks the guilt that oozes from his skin like a cheap cologne. "This fresh air is killing me."

I sit down next to him. "Maybe another cigarette will help."

"I'd prefer a shot of tequila."

"Why do you hit the bottle so hard?"

Alex is silent for a minute. "I never drank much till five years ago. My son Toby was killed. He ran out into the street after our dog and was hit by a car. He died three days before his fourth birthday."

Suddenly, my old age seems minor.

"I didn't even cry at his funeral," he says. "I only missed one day of work. I wish I could say that about all the drinking. My boss gave me time off to dry out. I'm the best mechanic in the shop but not much of a husband."

"Neither am I."

"You're not supposed to outlive your children," he says. "My wife and I never talk about it."

"Christy lost two babies to miscarriage. I can't imagine losing a four-year-old."

"I blamed my wife, but it was my fault too. I was at work in the garage. I should have kept an eye on Toby. The guilt never goes away. I just drown it with booze."

"How's your wife?"

"She took our daughter and moved in with her mom. If I don't sober up, I'll lose her."

"I don't know if Christy wants me back. I need to pull myself together, and fast."

"I don't know if I have the strength…" his voice trails off.

Eli calls from the other end of the park. "It's four o'clock guys. Time to head back."

• • •

A loud scream echoes down the hall. Sandy runs out of her room wearing only a towel draped across her chest and thighs. Water drips off her legs and her hair is covered with pink puffs of shampoo. It's the first time I've seen her without her pajamas.

Someone yells out, "Hello, beautiful." Sandy frantically clutches her towel and runs head long into Mary, who whisks her into the counseling office.

Following the crowd down the hall, I peek into Sandy's bathroom. Alex, pale and shivering, hugs the toilet. The water is still running in the shower. Maru turns it off and stands over Alex. "Exactly what are you doing?"

"What does it look like?" Alex says. He sticks his head in the bowl and heaves.

"You're in Sandy's bathroom. You're not allowed in here."

He looks up. "You mean this isn't the altar at St. Peter's Basilica?" He heaves in the bowl again.

"I'm giving you a warning this time, but if it happens again, you're in big trouble," Maru says. A subtle grin creeps onto his face. "Now, let's get you to the dispensary for some medicine."

• • •

Later that night at Evening Wrap Up, Nurse Lisa asks us to form a circle and apologize to someone for a past wrong. I ask for a pass to the bathroom.

"I'd like to apologize to my daughter," Sandy says. "I gave her up for adoption when I was sixteen and haven't seen her since."

I stand alone behind a locked door as the voices of contrition torment my ears.

"Are you OK?" Maru asks, as I walk back to the circle.

"Just nauseous."

I'm not ready to confess my sins.

"Did you and Alex take something while you were walking around the park?"

"Just a dose of self-reflection," I say.

It didn't go down well.

The meeting is about to end. "I want to say something," Alex says. His head is downcast as he walks over to Sandy, who fidgets in her chair.

"I want to apologize for running into your bathroom," Alex says. He stands stiffly with his hands in his pockets. "I thought it was my room. Sorry."

"It's OK. You were sick," Sandy says.

"I thought I was having another hallucination when I saw you in the shower. You were the best one I've had all week."

Chapter 38

I hear blood curdling screams in my sleep that night as the lioness clamps her powerful jaws over the nose of the terrified young wildebeest and slowly suffocates it while other members of the pride tear chunks of meat from its hindquarter. My bladder is about to burst but I'm not leaving my bed. I'm not the top of the food chain in this brutish primitive place. I tuck myself deeper into the safety of my burrow. An insect scampers across my face. I reach up to flick it off when a dozen more trickle down my neck. I sweep them off, but in seconds my skin crawls with fire ants. Their stingers puncture my flesh and inject a venom that burns like hot oil. I'm startled awake to find my sweat drenched sheet pulled over my head.

"Are you OK?" Charles asks.

It was just a nightmare.

"I'm fine," I say.

• • •

At therapy class, Gina sits in a corner by the door with her back to the wall. Her long legs sprawl out like the metal legs of the chair and her black leather boots twitch. She glances over at the window to the parking lot.

"I want each of you to think about something that makes you anxious," Carson says. "Gina, tell us what makes you nervous."

Gina is silent.

"How about talking in public?" Carson says.

I'm afraid I'll get insomnia and go crazy again.

"A bit," Gina says.

"Anything else?"

No response.

"How about people you don't know?" Carson asks.

"Sure."

"Think of the last time you felt anxious about strangers, Gina."

Gina pauses for a moment. "When first I arrived at the clinic and saw all the patients at dinner." We are a scary looking bunch of screwballs.

"Describe what that was like."

"It was like the bar scene from *Star Wars.*"

"Yeah, with all those reptile creatures," Alex blurts out. Larry looked like the one playing the saxophone.

"I think the same thing when I come into the clinic some days," Carson says, smiling. "What makes you so nervous?"

"I'm waiting to see who's going to pull a knife."

I pulled a knife on those cops.

"Gina, how many days have you been in the clinic?"

"Ten."

"And how many knife fights have you witnessed during those ten days?"

"None."

"Would you say the chance of someone pulling a knife in the clinic is a low or a high probability event?"

"It could happen."

Maybe Gina's not so crazy.

"Yes," Carson says, "but is it low or high probability?"

"Low, but it happened to me. I was stabbed in the back by an inmate."

Maybe Gina embezzled funds.

"OK, but that was in a women's prison where you were a guard on duty. This is a psychiatric clinic and you're here as a patient. It's a different setting."

No way! She's a prison guard?

"It doesn't feel different," Gina says.

"Remember what I said earlier in the week. Our brains are hard wired to look for danger. It's our flight or fight response. The caveman that missed the lion did not survive, so we constantly search for lions, like your attack in the prison. Now you see lions everywhere. Does that make sense?"

"I think so."

Christy's never going to trust me now.

Worrying about a low probability event," Carson says, "will cause stress."

"How do I stop?"

She'll always worry that I might go crazy.

"Stay locked in your present setting. If your mind slips into the past, refocus."

I'm never going to be able to sleep in the same bed with her.

"I'll try," Gina says.

I've lost her, forever.

CHAPTER 39

Alex stands by the door to the smoking lawn and watches several patients puff away outside. His thumbs are tucked in the front pockets of his jeans, the four fingers of each hand quiver. Alex is a puzzle. He's the court jester in our royal nuthouse. One minute he's a junkyard dog taking a piss; the next minute he's a circus monkey riding a scooter.

"I would die for a smoke right now."

"Join them. Light up."

"I can't. I quit."

"Why?"

"Pollutes my lungs."

"I've got an ice cream bar stashed in the back of the freezer. You want it?"

"Bad for my cholesterol."

"You're an alcoholic in detox who smokes and you're worried an ice cream bar will ruin your health."

"I'll take it."

I hand it to him. He takes one bite and throws it in a garbage basket by the door.

"Is this part of your penance?" I ask.

"What?" he says, a blank look on his face.

"You know, self-mortification for a past sin."

He winces. "My mom didn't believe in sin." He picks the ice cream bar out of the trash and takes a bite.

"What if you didn't do your chores?"

"I never had any." He slides the bar into his back pocket. He doesn't notice my raised eyebrow.

"That must have been fun, growing up without rules," I say.

"It doesn't work. I can't say no."

"I've had years of practice. You'll get the hang of it."

"If you're so good at saying no," Alex says, "how come you tried to off yourself."

"I can't handle the thought of getting old and dying," I say.

"I've got news flash for you, buddy. Nobody's getting out of here alive."

A piece of ice cream dribbles onto the floor beneath Alex's feet. I point to it.

"Shit!" Alex says. He pulls the blob out of his pocket. It flops on the floor. We stare at it.

"You're afraid of dying so you tried to commit suicide," he says. He scoops the lump of ice cream up off the floor and dumps it back in the trash bin, wiping his hands on his white cotton tee shirt.

"This comes from a guy who admits he is a mean drunk," I say.

"True, but the prick who ran over my son never spent a day in jail."

"I thought it was an accident."

"You don't get it, do you?"

I step back. His face convulses. "Get what?"

"I was the driver," he says. "I killed Toby."

I have no reply.

Alex runs down the hall, leaving me alone. I walk slowly back to my room and stand over the sink. I'm humbled. He shared his darkest heartache with me.

CHAPTER 40

Looking in the mirror, an avalanche of memory sweeps me off my feet. I crumble to the bathroom floor.

It was three days before I first entered the clinic, before I'd ever met Alex. I hadn't slept in six nights. My cell phone rang. I grabbed it. All I heard was a dial tone.

Was I losing touch with reality? The thought terrified me. I wanted the piercing pain in my chest to go away, fast. I knew how. The crystal-clear waters of Lake Tahoe would envelop me in an icy embrace. I would only struggle for a minute.

For several days Christy and I danced around the house, hot tubbed under the moonlight and made love. I wanted her to remember the good times when I was gone.

On Wednesday morning, I drove Christy over to Eagle Falls on the west shore of Lake Tahoe. It was her favorite hike. The sunlight streamed through towering Sugar pines and thawed a frozen layer of morning dew that crunched under our feet. Christy and I scrambled up the rugged granite trail towards the crackle of water crashing on bedrock. I stopped to catch my breath, the scent of pine cones and moss filled my lungs. My knee and back screamed at me, but I just bit my lip. Christy grabbed my hand and pulled me up the frosty cobblestones to the overlook.

"Come on, slowpoke. Since when do I have to drag you up a steep trail? You're always the mountain goat."

I was dead from lack of sleep. "I'm trying to digest that cinnamon roll I ordered with my cheese and sausage omelet," I said, holding my stomach in feigned misery.

"I offered you half my Avocado Benedict," Christy said.

Below us sheets of water cascaded down the tumbled slabs into a shimmering pool. Crusty slabs of granite protruded like scaly alligator heads out of the water. Above the falls patches of snow melted on the craggy face of Maggie's peak. The runoff formed ribbons that slithered down through grey rock fields to feed the forest surrounding Eagle Lake.

"Look, there's a marmot," she said, pointing to a fuzzy ball crawling down the rocks. On cue the marmot stood at attention and stared down at us with his head cocked.

I was spent. I couldn't keep up the charade much longer.

"You look tired," Christy said.

"I'm fine. I'll race you to the truck," I said, hobbling down the trail.

"Loser has to clean dishes for a week," Christy yelled. She bounded past me, her blond hair swirling down her back.

"No fair," I said, making a halfhearted attempt to catch her. Just above the parking lot my friend Andy chased his golden retriever in the creek bed. I waved. He didn't see me. No one would care if I disappeared.

Gasping for breath, I reached the truck. Christy sat on the tailgate, wearing a grin. She knew I hated doing dishes.

"Alright, I'll load the dishwasher, but you have to put them away."

"No way, you have to load and put everything away."

I could see I would lose this one. "OK."

"Are you sure you're all right?" I never gave up that easy.

"It's just a headache," I said. "I'll grab an aspirin from the glove box."

"OK, wait while I use the restroom."

I unlocked the truck and collapsed on the driver's seat. My head rested on the black leather steering wheel. All alone, the ache in my chest bubbled out my skin. Sweat dripped from my eyebrows and splattered the muddy carpet at my feet. The last vestiges of hope drained out my pores. I can't last another night. I watched the white capped waves lap against the rocks four hundred feet below. Only a thin band of steel stopped a car from flying off the cliff.

Wrapped up deep in my own despair, it made perfect sense. "I'm brave," I thought, though I was scared of dying. There is no other way out.

I started the truck.

The side door opened. "What's the hurry?" Christy asked, jumping in the cab.

No. Get out! I don't want you to get hurt.

Christy smiled and offered me her left cheek to kiss.

A sudden primal rage consumed me like a climax fire sending walls of fury leaping from tree top to tree top incinerating all my reason and self-control. I transformed into a delirious animal trapped by the flames blazing around me.

What happened next, I cannot explain.

I bared my teeth and bit into the soft flesh on her face. She screamed, touched her cheek and stared at the blood on her fingertips, her eyes void of all understanding. I straight armed the door and pushed her out of the cab. Blood splattered the pavement.

An overwhelming sense of emptiness enveloped me. There's no going back now.

I punched the gas pedal to the floor and aimed for a mangled section of guardrail five-hundred yards away, where avalanches careened off the cliffs above. Accelerating towards the lake, I saw my mother next to me, gripping the wheel of my Mustang. The pickets of the guardrail flew past.

"What are you doing here?" She seemed so real. I reached over to touch her but my hand passed through her arm.

"Don't worry," she said with a serene look. "You're not going to end up like Daniel."

Everything moved in slow motion. The oncoming cars swerved to avoid a head on collision. I could see the look of shock and dismay on the faces of each passenger as they slid past. Moments before the truck hit the railing, mom reached over and jerked the steering wheel out of my hands. The truck slammed sideways against the guardrail. A stream of sparks flew over the hood. A cloud of white exploded in my face and I waited for the soothing waters to swallow me.

When I came to, my truck was still entangled in the mangled metal railing. Cars zoomed past, horns screeching. I opened the door and staggered onto the asphalt. My legs collapsed. Someone dragged my limp body to the shoulder of the roadway.

"Erik, what happened? Are you alright?" It was Andy.

My jaw seized, my voice dead. Broken fragments of conversation drifted past.

"He's not violent. I've known him for thirty years."

"He assaulted his wife in the parking lot. We'll have to restrain him."

"Chief says strap him down."

I struggled against the talons that crushed my ankles and wrists. Blackness smothered me and my writhing body was carried off into the sky.

CHAPTER 41

I slowly pick myself off the cold concrete floor of the bathroom. As the memory of what I'd done to Christy floods my mind, I stare at the sad old man crying in the mirror. I strip naked and step into the shower. The scalding hot water won't rinse away my shame.

CHAPTER 42

Carson quietly opens the door for the afternoon therapy class and waves everyone in.

"Good afternoon, Charles. Hello Sandy. Hi, Gina, Alex."

I wait at the end of the line, impressed that he remembers everyone's names. "Good afternoon, Erik," he says, patting my hand. Glancing down, I look for a list of names written in ink on his wrist, but find only a cheap chrome watch.

"Do you have time to talk later today?"

"Of course, meet me at my office an hour after class."

"Thanks."

Carson is earnest in his efforts to patch up the battle-scarred troops that get helicoptered in and out of his ward. Wearing neatly pressed trousers, a crisp shirt and tie, his face is calm. His training, listening to patients pour out their troubles without reaction, provides him with a mask of neutrality, but I can see through his body armor. A pale ring of flesh is visible from his missing wedding band.

Carson hands out paper and pencils all around.

"I want each of you to write down what's important in your life."

I stare at the blank sheet in front of me for several minutes.

"Charles, what do you value?" Carson asks.

"Kindness," he says.

"Sandy?"

"Honesty."

"Gina, what motivates you to get out of bed every day."

"My son, Noah."

While Carson circles the room questioning the patients, I gaze out the window and watch a woman in a hair net and kitchen smock argue with the driver of a food truck as he unloads boxes from the back of the cargo hold. He's big, six inches taller and twice her size, tough looking and thoroughly outmatched. She jabs him in his belly, backing him up with each poke of her finger until he raises his arms over head like he's getting robbed at gunpoint. I make a note never to piss off the kitchen staff.

I look over to see, **Laughter**, **Honesty, Friends, Family, Kindness** and **God** written across the whiteboard.

"This is worse than Sunday school," Alex whispers to me. He doesn't hear what Carson preaches. He only hears the screams of his son.

"Erik," Carson asks, "what's the most important thing in your life?

"My wife."

"Now write down what you did to end up here in the clinic," Carson says.

I pick up the pencil. My right hand convulses. I can't write down in black and white what I did to Christy and show the world a domestic violence report on a police blotter. I set the pencil down.

"Sandy, you go first."

Sandy squirms in her seat.

"I have an eating disorder."

I look down and watch in amazement as my hand grabs the pencil and it glides across the paper.

"I starve myself then binge and purge," she says.

My hand moves on its own accord.

"Is that in keeping with your core value of honesty?" Carson asks.

"I tell myself food is making me fat when it's keeping me alive."

When my hand stops, I read the words: **"I tried to commit suicide. I assaulted my wife."**

Chapter 43

"Erik."

My eyes open. Carson is tapping me on the arm.

"Sorry, I drifted off."

"What brought you into the clinic?"

"I assaulted my wife." I retch and start to sob.

Carson squats down next to me and massages my neck, and then says to the group, "Let's take a short break." Patients stream out into the hall behind him. It's only the two of us now.

"I remembered my suicide attempt. I attacked Christy. How could I have done that?"

"You were psychotic from lack of sleep."

"I love her."

"Then you need to heal yourself."

I lean over and give Carson a hug. He lets me hold him for a minute as my tears slow to a trickle and run dry.

Alex walks in the door. Carson stands up and returns to the front of the room.

"Next time, rent a hotel room," Alex says as he sits down.

• • •

A few minutes later, the classroom is full.

"Everyone makes mistakes," Carson says. "If you acknowledge, take responsibility and come to peace with them; you'll grow."

"That sounds very Zen Buddhist," Charles says.

"You don't need to follow any religion. Forgiveness is universal. Can anybody give me a quote on forgiveness?" Carson asks.

"My mother always mentioned a passage in the bible, 'Forgive and you will be forgiven,'" Sandy says.

"The first step to forgive yourself is to realize the person you are dealing with is a complete idiot," I say.

"Good," Carson says.

"There's no problem so awful that you can't add some guilt to it and make it even worse,"[6] Gina says.

"Anyone else?" Carson asks.

"Alex?"

His tortured soul is too wounded. "This is bullshit!" Alex shouts. He storms out the door, leaving Carson confused.

He can't face himself. Neither could I. That's why I had amnesia. I need to call Christy.

• • •

I get permission to use the phone after class. "Hi, honey. How are you?"

"I've been having trouble sleeping," she says.

"That's my fault."

"I'm sorry I told the police you assaulted me."

"You did the right thing."

"How are you doing?" she asks.

"I remembered what I did to you at Eagle Falls."

If I really love her, maybe I should let her go.

"I don't know how much more of this I can take," she says.

"I can't do this on my own," I say. "I need help. I need to stay here for a while."

"I know that's hard for you to admit."

"I lied about my medication. I'm done lying."

"I should have told you about the house. I know how important it is to you."

"We can live in our tent. Cash would love it. I can design Cash his own cardboard doghouse. We can sleep on the bike path along the Truckee river. I'll panhandle while you work at the hospital."

A tiny smile trickles across the phone line. Maybe I can win her back.

"Get better this time," Christy says.

CHAPTER 44

Carson stands at his desk when I enter his office. "Sit down. You had a big breakthrough today." I settle into the chair as he closes his computer screen and sits across from me.

"I couldn't face the truth. That's why I had amnesia."

"It was an intense emotional trauma. You needed time to absorb it."

"I don't understand why Christy took me back."

"She was willing to forgive you."

"Not now."

"She's seems very compassionate. You'll have to see."

"Will we ever get back to normal?"

"After a suicide attempt or assault, you'll find you're not the same."

"So, the old Erik flew off the cliff into Lake Tahoe?" I say.

"You've evolved. We all do. There's no going back."

"Christy won't ever forget what I did."

"I had a music teacher in third grade, Mrs. Mullins. She told me my voice was off key in front of the whole class. I was so embarrassed. I still remember my trauma, but the emotion is gone. If you and Christy are willing to let it go, your suicide attempt and Christy's memory of the assault will lose their emotional impact. It will take time and a lot of grace."

Moments are etched in the arc of my life, scattered and unexpected. A spark. A point of contact. Unbridled joy and searing pain. It can be as simple as a smile when she awakes or as piercing as her scream. Each one is intimate. The fear in her eyes when she crashes on the asphalt. The sweet taste of her lips when I collapse in her arms. The scent of her hair lingers. I slip back into my shell.

Christy, Joe, Mom, Dad, Daniel. These are the deepest ones. Daniel and Dad fell into the abyss. Mom and Christy slip from my grasp. That is why I cling.

"I'll hope you're right," I say. "So, you don't spend your Saturday nights at Karaoke bars."

"No, my teacher was right. I'm a terrible singer," Carson says.

Chapter 45

Gina sticks her head in our room as Charles and I are getting ready for dinner. "Alex has cancer."

"What are you talking about?" I ask.

"He went for some tests last week, complaining about his stomach. Dr. Williams called him into his office. They take him back to the hospital tomorrow."

"How could he have cancer?" I say. "He's in his twenties."

"One of my son's classmates has battled leukemia since first grade," Gina says.

My back and knee problems suddenly seem trivial.

The dining room buzzes with the news when we arrive. Alex emerges from Carson's office and slumps into a chair between Gina and Sandy. They lean over and hug him.

"What did the doctors say?" Sandy asks.

"I have a tumor. They want to do a CT scan to see if it's spread."

"What then?" I ask.

"Surgery in a day or two. Dr. Williams says they have a high rate of success with this form of cancer."

"You're young," Charles says. "Your body will fight for you."

"You can have my pizza, if you want," Sandy says, sliding her plate to John. He doesn't respond. His tumor isn't hungry.

"I leave at seven AM tomorrow," he says. He drops his head into his hands.

"I'm a cancer survivor," Gina says. "The initial shock is the worst."

"Did you have chemo?" Alex asks.

"No, just radiation after the surgery," Gina says. She punches him in the shoulder. "Hey, if a girl can deal with cancer, how hard can it be?" Alex winces.

Gina points to her breasts, "They're fake. The real ones tried to kill me."

• • •

After dinner, I call Joe.

"I'm at the hospice with Mom."

"Put her on the line." I say.

"I don't know; she's pretty disoriented."

"Let me just say hi." Mom is close to the end of her journey. The cobbles fall away beneath her. I hide in the gutter, watching her pass, embarrassed to show her my tattered soul.

I hear the phone being fumbled and a faint, "Hello."

"Hi, Mom."

"Daniel?"

"This is Erik."

"Where's Daniel?"

Chapter 46

It was a Saturday morning. President John F. Kennedy had been assassinated three weeks earlier in Dallas and Daniel was due home for the weekend. He was a freshman at Loyola University and lived on campus in Westchester, a suburb of LA. Joe and I watched TV. Everyone else on the block had a color TV, but ours was black and white. Mom said we could make do with what we had.

"Come and get it," Mom yelled. "Breakfast is ready."

"We'll be there in a minute," I said. We were watching Superman. Lois Lane's car was stopped dead on the railroad tracks.

Joe lay on the floor, his face three feet from the screen, sucking his thumb. I bit my fingernails on the couch behind him. We were glued to the tube. We sat through an Oscar Meyer Weiner commercial, waiting for the climactic rescue.

"Erik, turn off the boob tube," Mom yelled. "Breakfast is getting cold."

"It's almost over."

Mom walked into the living room. She scowled.

"I said turn it off, this minute."

"Please?"

Marching across the room, she yanked the TV plug out of the wall.

"Bag your head." she yelled, "and go eat your breakfast."

We followed her into the kitchen. The phone rang. Mom left us to skulk, staring at our steaming bowls of oatmeal. I heard crying in the den. Mom never cried, even at Dad's funeral. Joe and I ran to her. She grabbed me in one arm and Joe in the other.

"What's wrong?" I asked.

"Daniel's in the hospital."

"Can we go see him?" I asked.

"No," Mom said, wiping the tears from her cheek.

"Why not? He's our brother," Joe said.

"Children aren't allowed." She led us back into the kitchen. We sat down at the table, Mom in between us.

"Daniel felt so sick he couldn't get out of bed. They've taken him to this special hospital so he can rest."

It didn't make any sense. Daniel was big and strong. Maybe someone put kryptonite under his bed.

"I need to go see Daniel," Mom said, "Erik, can you take care of Joe for a few hours?" I didn't want Mom to leave.

"I'll ask the neighbors to stop by and check on you," Mom said. "You can watch TV if you want."

My eyes lit up.

Mom spent every Saturday morning for the next year visiting Daniel. She always went alone. I realize now how devastating that was for her; the first cracks were forming. I became the man of the house that winter. Joe and I walked up to the public library one Saturday morning and looked up schizophrenia. We decided Daniel went crazy because he wasn't the smartest kid in school anymore.

• • •

I hold my hand over the phone while I choke back tears. "Daniel's not here, Mom." I say. I should have listened to Joe.

"You need to rest, Mom." Joe says. "We'll talk to Erik another time."

Joe comes back on the line. "She's having a rough day."

"I didn't mean to upset her." I share my grief with passing strangers and hide it from the woman who brought me into this world.

"She knows. How are you doing?"

"I talked to Christy and apologized."

"Good. Open up to her. She's stronger than you think."

"I'm afraid I'll lose her."

"You will if you keep hiding things."

CHAPTER 47

At Evening Wrap Up, Alex sits slumped over in his chair getting a neck massage from Nurse Lisa. The room is listless. The parched air wilts my concentration and everyone is limp as they take turns describing their successes and failures for the day. Our small strides and stumbles seem trifling, cracks in the sidewalk compared to the gaping canyon Alex is trying to traverse.

When everyone else is done, Alex stands up. His voice is frail.

"For the last four hours, I've been asking God why he's doing this to me. I don't want to die." His face shatters like a plate hitting a concrete floor. There's a minute of silence as he picks up the loose shards scattered across the room. "This is a wakeup call. No more alcohol. I've learned my lesson. If I survive, I'm not wasting another day."

His voice shrivels and evaporates into dust.

PART FOUR

"You're mad, bonkers, completely off your head.
But I'll tell you a secret. All the best people are."[7]

CHAPTER 48

2:00 am. The covers rustle across the room and in the shadows, I watch Charles wrestle with his own maleficent spirits. He tosses and turns and mumbles in a language I don't understand. The words are garbled and squished together, beaten and strangled by the phantoms of the night, till they slowly shrivel and disappear. I am alone again, listening to the soft cadence of my pulsing heart. I say a few prayers for Alex, hoping he will win his battle, and reflect on my mom and this young man both fighting cancer. Sturdy saplings and ancient oaks ripped from the soil. At least my mom was granted a full, productive life. I can't explain the random nature of their shared predicament. Why is one tree left standing in a pool of sadness, branches battered, leaves stripped bare?

Everyone in the clinic struggles to deal with their personal issues. As I float on my mattress on a storm-less sea, I realize this is the first night in months I haven't been overwhelmed by my own private demons. My gorilla has been muted by my words of contrition and compassion for another lost soul. Drifting off to sleep, I hear Alex whisper in my ear, "I'm not wasting another day."

• • •

For the next eight weeks, I grind my way through the daily regimen of psychic pushups, commitment calisthenics, pills, pancakes and pizza. I endure intensely humbling and naked moments of self-reflection that make me stagger on my feet and crushing nights of guilt and fear that find me quaking in my sheets. Carson's insights and meditation, Dr. William's medication, and the wisecracks, wisdom and weeping from my fellow grunts carries me through this boot camp for the emotionally 4-F in our nut hut Quonset hut. We're psychiatric amputees being fitted for new prosthetic souls and learning to walk again. It's no five-star soul spa. It's a gritty, chaotic, intense and sometimes morbid painting of human frailty and failure, dappled with splashes of resilience and courage. I spend thirty minutes a day on the solitary exercise bike, listening to the same broken wheel bearing click with each rotation of the pedal. Sandy, Charles, Alex and Gina are long gone. Every day a new batch of rookies arrive on stretchers and stare, blank and shell shocked at the whiteboard. I feel like a grizzled veteran. I talk to Christy and Joe twice a week. Christy hasn't slammed down the phone in over a month. Mom hangs on, to the amazement of her doctors and to my huge relief. I've been thinking a lot about what may be my last words to her.

When Dr. Williams tells me I'm ready for discharge, I'm terrified and elated at the same time. Whatever happens, I'm determined to follow my heart. The real word beckons. Christy is picking me up. I won't ever forget this screwball sanitarium.

Chapter 49

Maru opens the security door and both Joe and Christy appear. There are strands of white in the wave of her hair. The soft beige makeup dusting her face can't quite hide the circular scar on her left cheek. Her face is weary but composed. She smiles weakly. Joe pulls off his aviator sunglasses, exposing bloodshot eyes, and drops them into the pocket of his wrinkled dress shirt.

He feigns a forward lunge then hugs me.

"Joe, I didn't know you were coming," I say. He's here to protect Christy.

"I flew into Reno early this morning. I wanted to be here." I would do the same.

I kiss Christy gently, careful to avoid her camouflaged wound.

"How are you?" she asks.

"I'm nervous and humbled; this is the hardest thing I've ever done."

Joe jabs my chest. "You're looking fit."

"It's my new nutritional program, the suicidal depression diet. It's like Jenny Craig, but you eat prepackaged servings of bummer, funk, and gloom instead of breakfast, lunch, and dinner."

"Then you're due for a good meal. Where do you want to grab lunch?"

"How about a burrito at T's Rotisserie?" I say.

"Don't you want to go someplace fancy to celebrate?" Christy asks.

"I don't need fancy. I've got you two," I say.

• • •

When we reach the parking lot, I see Cash bark excitedly from the back of my pickup, his tail spinning at hypersonic helicopter speed. "I missed you too, buddy," I say. He licks my face but I hear no response. Thank God, I've got that behind me.

"Do you mind if I ride in the open bed with Cash?" I ask as we exit the clinic. "I've been cooped up for the last eight weeks."

Joe and Christy look at one another. "I just want some fresh air."

"Ok," they say in unison.

Cash and I lean our heads over the side of the truck as we climb past hillsides speckled with Utah junipers twisted by the wind into oversize bonsai sculptures and mountain mahogany sprinkled with wispy white seed tails that corkscrew off the boughs and decorate the shrubs like flocking on a Christmas tree. Approaching the summit, I see a ragged figure standing on the side of the highway with his thumb out. As we pass, I recognize the denim jacket.

"Pull over!" I say, pounding on the hood of the truck. Joe eases onto the shoulder of the road as Larry approaches.

"Are you sure you want to pick this guy up?" Joe says. "He looks pretty scruffy."

"I know him," I say. Joe shakes his head in disbelief.

"Hop in, Larry." I say, dropping the tail gate. I reach out my hand. "Where are you going?"

Larry crawls onto the bed. "Do I know you?" he asks.

"Erik, from the clinic." Cash rubs his nose on Larry's palm.

"Oh," he says. "Nice dog." He bends over and scratches Cash behind the ears. Joe accelerates back onto the roadway.

"Where to?" I ask again.

"Incline."

"What for?"

"Food."

"Where are you staying?" I ask.

"The woods."

"In what?"

"A tent." Larry isn't much on conversation. Neither was Daniel, after he came back from the hospital. We sit quietly and watch the towering pines along the road fly past. It's calming, but I wonder if life is passing me by.

"Here!" Larry says.

I tap on the rear window of the truck and Joe pulls over. There's a line formed next to a truck that reads Project MANA, the local food bank. Larry rolls off the side of the truck and steps to the back of the line. He turns and nods. Joe drives off.

I've been hiding in the woods like Larry for the last two years.

• • •

I hold the door open for Christy and Joe when we enter the restaurant. The flames from the mesquite rotisserie flicker in the background and fill the air with the rich aroma of Yucatan spices and orange slices. We order at the counter and I lead us to a corner table to shield our conversation from the prying ears of the other patrons. I'm not ready to share my faults with the world.

"I spoke with the Placer County district attorney," Joe says.

"If I need to go to jail for what I did, it's OK," I say.

Christy flinches. She could have been seriously hurt, or worse.

"That won't be necessary," Joe says. "I took a letter from Dr. Williams to the DA and he decided not to press charges." I put her life in danger when I pulled out the knife.

"I told him I wouldn't testify against you," Christy says. She cups her hands around the salt shaker, her eyes downcast.

"You did the right thing to call the police," I say. She looks up briefly and blinks away a small tear.

"The DA's office will need monthly letters from Dr. Williams to confirm your outpatient treatment is ongoing and current," Joe says. The steaming hot burritos arrive, filled with succulent chicken, Cuban black beans, bubbling cheese, fresh pico de gallo, guacamole and sour cream. I've craved a killer burrito for weeks.

"I have my appointment calendar filled out for the next six months," I say.

"Good. We need to leave right away to see Mom," Joe says.

I'm not ready. "I want to spend some time with Christy." I reach under the table and put my hand on Christy's knee. She puts her hand on mine.

"She doesn't respond when I talk to her." Joe says. "Sister Gertrude thinks she's in the final stages," My appetite vanishes.

The waitress comes by to pick up Christy and Joe's empty plates. I ask for a doggie bag.

"We have plane reservations on the 8:00 pm flight into Burbank," Joe says.

Chapter 50

The wind dances through the grove of aspen trees behind the house when we pull in our driveway. Wispy leaves the size of silver dollars flutter in the breeze like the wings on a butterfly. Two Calliope hummingbirds chase one another, zipping straight up in the air in an acrobatic combat display worthy of the Blue Angels. Another hummingbird dashes between the red trumpet flowers of the scarlet Gilia. It hovers like a helicopter with his black needle beak drawing nectar from base of the flower tube.

The blue flax and Sierra columbine have gone to seed. The summer bloom fades and my homecoming is bitter-sweet. I'm losing my house and my mom. My marriage is about to drift off in the wind. I have only three hours before Joe and I leave. Christy and I take a walk around the garden.

"I can't leave you," I say.

"I can't see your Mom like that."

"What happened to your blue lupine?" I ask, pointing to the withered stalks keeled over and cradling the dirt.

"The voles have eaten their roots." Christy reaches down and casually pulls up two brown stems.

"Shall I get out our old vole traps?" I ask. Christy drops the withered lupine in the dirt.

"Don't bother. The field mice eat weeds and snails and fertilize the soil. I offer them a few lupine in return. Only ten percent of their pups survive a month."

"Are you sure you don't want to come with me?" I ask.

"I'll just be in your way." Christy says.

"Your field mice missed some weeds over here," I say, pointing to fresh shoots under the Canyon maple tree.

"Those are Sulphur buckwheat, one of my favorite wildflowers." Christy says. "The seeds migrated in with the wind, just like the golden poppies at our feet."

"Where did they come from?" I ask.

"See those flowers down the street," Christy says, pointing across a wide expanse of asphalt.

"That's at least two hundred yards away."

"I tried to organize the yard into zones, but every year the wildflowers sneak across my artificial lines of demarcation and form their own neighborhoods."

We step over the bed of cobbles winding through our garden and approach a dozen brilliant red wildflowers nestled among a tuft of green fescue grass.

"I used to pull all the grass, but the Indian paintbrush can't survive without a host. Their roots graft onto the fescue to draw moisture and nutrients from them."

I'm like the paintbrush, I need Christy to survive.

"Will you be here when I get back," I ask.

"Go see your mom," she says.

"So, grass is OK here?"

"I tolerate a few clumps for my paintbrush. We aren't best friends."

"What about dandelions?" I ask, pointing to the spikey green weed with a yellow head of ray florets hidden beside her feet.

Christy bends down and yanks the intruder from the soil.

"I eat them," she says, munching on the leaves.

As we walk back to the house, Christy bends over and kisses me on the cheek. "I'll wait for you." she says, "but not forever."

Christy's garden constantly evolves. It changes despite her efforts to maintain control. She has made peace with the unpredictable mutations of her sanctuary. I hope she will be more forgiving with me than she is with her dandelions.

CHAPTER 51

After packing my bag, I take ten minutes to wade through the pile of mail on my desk. I'm embarrassed to see several get-well cards. I open the first one when the phone rings.

"Erik, you wacko, how was your stay in the funny farm?"

It's my old college roommate, Michael. He always makes me laugh. I can tell this is not going to be an intimate exchange of shared emotional trauma and decide to go with the flow.

"Great, I'm writing up a review on Yelp. I can't decide if the electroshock treatment was worth three or four stars. Hold on, I'm having another flashback." I rap the phone down on my desk top like I'm playing a drum solo for a heavy metal band. "Definitely four stars," I say, "and as a bonus, I can plug a phone jack in my tush and recharge my cell phone in five minutes flat."

"I was never offered electroshock treatment," Michael says.

"What are you talking about?"

"After my divorce, I went on Lexapro and saw a therapist for four years."

I shake my head in disbelief. "You never told me."

"I never told anyone."

I never had a clue.

"That's something I'm trying to change, to open up." Michael says.

"Guys don't," I say.

"Teddy Roosevelt, Isaac Newton, Charles Darwin and Abraham Lincoln all suffered from depression."

"Good to know I'm not the only one," I say.

"I'll call you in a week," he says.

He hangs up the phone. I could use more friends like Michael.

• • •

Christy drops Joe and me at the Reno airport. "Tell your mom I love her, will you?" she says.

"Of course," I say. I hug her tightly.

Joe and I wind our way through the maze of ticket counters, luggage drops and security checks and arrive at the departure gate with time to spare. We sit down opposite the slot machines that run down the center of the waiting area like the column of a marching band, their neon lights flashing in time to a John Phillip Souza tune.

"How are you and Christy doing?" Joe asks, putting his arm on my shoulder.

"She's still traumatized," I say.

"She's one in a million. Don't let her go." His arm grips me tight.

And to think I was going to abandon Joe and leave Christy all alone by killing myself.

• • •

"That's us," I say when the loudspeaker announces our plane is boarding. After giving my pass to the attendant, I follow Joe down the jet bridge to the plane.

"Do you remember that hike Mom took us on across the Grand Canyon?" I say.

"That wasn't a hike. That was a forced march," Joe says. We stand in the aisle and wait for the passengers ahead of us to stow their bags.

"I can still see those tourists on donkeys that we passed climbing up the north rim."

"What did she call them?"

"Slackers on hay burners," I say.

We find our seats and buckle in.

"I was afraid she would get arrested," Joe says.

"She never should have told them to get off their asses and clean up the road apples."

We laugh. The stewardess shows us the safety features of the Boeing 737 jet.

"The thought of losing Mom makes me feel mortal," Joe says.

The stewardess stops to bring Joe's seat forward for takeoff. He barely notices her smile.

"I feel guilty for not being at her side for the last two months," I say.

Joe looks tired. "You're shooting yourself with a second arrow." He's shouldered all the burden.

"What's that mean?" I ask.

"Mom's dying. That's the first arrow. Your guilt is the second," Joe says.

"Since when have you become a Buddhist monk?" I ask.

"I went on a Zen retreat while you were in the clinic." The jet taxis a short distance and stops, waiting for clearance.

"What did you learn?"

"Two things. First, if I accept that mom is dying, I can be there for her. If I resist, I just make myself miserable."

"You're a great brother, Joe." I sit silently for a few seconds. "What's the second one?"

"My butt goes numb after meditating for two hours."

Chapter 52

"You grab our luggage and I'll meet you at the passenger loading zone," Joe says as we walk through the Burbank airport.

"OK. Give me your luggage tag," I say.

Twenty minutes later, I wave and Joe pulls his BMW M6 convertible alongside the curb, stopping just inches from my foot. I throw the bags in the backseat and hop in.

"You've watched over Mom for the last two months. I'll cover for you tonight. Just drop me off at the hospice center and go home," I say.

"Are you sure?" Joe says.

"It's my turn. You need a good night's rest."

• • •

A large wooden cross hangs above the front door of the Sisters of Mercy Hospice Center. The hinges creak as I pull the heavy timber door open. Inside the entry, I notice an arched alcove on my left. A smiling statue of the Blessed Mary floats on a glass shelf flooded in light that spills down to a beige couch. A white-haired woman in a black nun's habit and running shoes walks briskly towards me. She appears to have wings on her feet, but I realize it's just the swoosh on her sneakers.

"How can I help you?" she says.

"I'm here to see my mother, Harriet Scott."

"You must be Erik. I'm Sister Gertrude. I'm so glad you were able to make it."

"How's she doing?"

"We have her on a morphine drip so she's not in any pain, but she stopped eating three days ago. I'm afraid she won't let go. She's waiting for you."

I follow the sister down a narrow corridor with immaculate white walls. It's quiet, except for the hum of the air conditioner spilling down from a grille in the ceiling. The chilled air sends a shiver along my bare arms. Sister Gertrude holds open the door to my mom's room.

"Thank you," I say. She nods and follows me in.

The room is dimly lit. Two pale green upholstered chairs nestle together in a far corner, hunched together like two sisters in prayer. A simple wooden nightstand sits at the head of the bed. A spray of red carnations sprouts out of a white vase that sits on top of the nightstand. A single tattered book perches next to the vase, frayed white stitching exposed by the peeled leather spine.

I grab one of the chairs and sit next to the bed. Two clear IV bags hang off a steel stand with tubes descending down like tentacles that disappear under the bed linens. In the center of the bed, I make out a tiny figure swathed in white sheets. My mother's face is gaunt and her eyes are closed, sunken deep into their sockets. The furrowed skin on her cheeks is pale, almost translucent. I trace the tubes of the IV to find her delicate hand and hold it in my palm. Her bony fingers are curled up in a ball and slightly cold to my touch.

"Hello, Mom."

"Is that you, Daniel?" she whispers.

"I'll leave you two alone," Sister Gertrude says, exiting the room, quietly closing the door behind her.

I lift a strand of white hair off my Mom's forehead. "No Mom, it's Erik.

"That's right, Daniel killed himself."

"That wasn't your fault." I lean over and kiss her on the cheek.

Should I tell her I share the same demons that took Daniel?

I gently cup my mother's wrinkled hand in both of my palms like I am holding a butterfly about to fly away.

"You're a terrific Mom."

"I love you," she says, gently squeezing my palm. Her head slips back onto the pillow. We sit in silence, our hands intertwined. I listen to the sound of her shallow breathing. It's labored, unsteady. I close my eyes and listen to the rhythmic flow of my own breath. We drift off to sleep to the sound of "May you be happy; may you find peace," echoing in my head.

I wake to a knock on the door.

"Come in," I say, lifting my head off the edge of the bed.

Sister Gertrude enters, rolling a cart with sponges, towels, blankets and two steel bowls filled with water. "It's time for your bath, Harriet."

Mom stirs and tries in vain to rise up from the bed. Her head barely moves off the pillow.

"Would you like to bath your mother?" she asks.

"I can help."

"Would that be OK, Harriet?" Sister asks.

Mom nods meekly, but her eyes remain closed. Does she understand?

Sister Gertrude and I pull back layers of white sheets that sandwich a soft beige blanket. She is swaddled in a cocoon of gossamer linen so transparent her shriveled shell is fully exposed. Her stomach is sunken, each rib protrudes; Mom has covered her bosom with her bony hands, but there's nothing to hide. They are only barren memories of the breasts that once nourished me. An oversize plastic diaper is her only clothing. Her tiny legs look so fragile they might shatter at any moment.

A nurse sticks her head in the door. "We need you at the front desk, Sister Gertrude," she says.

"You'll be OK doing this by yourself, won't you?" she says. Her steel blue eyes are unflinching, but serene.

Before I can protest, she's out the door.

I unwrap Mom from her linen cocoon and place a towel over her waist and legs. The sponge drips on the mattress as I swab my Mother's face, neck and shoulders. I detect a slight movement in her lips, but her words are barely whispers.

"I'm dying," she says.

I lean over and place my ear inches from her mouth.

"I'm sorry, Phillip," she says, then cringes.

I haven't heard Mom speak my father's name in fifty years.

Her face contorts with pain. "I never should have kicked you out."

I lift her emaciated arm and wipe the talcum powder from her armpit.

"I never talked to you about Dad," I say.

"I found his death certificate when I was nine."

The terry cloth towel is cold to my touch.

"Why, Phillip? Why suicide?" she asks.

"Joe and I knew he killed himself, but we never told you," I say.

I watch the skeletal remains of her chest rise and fall as I gently sponge her bare bosom.

"Sister Gertrude says you won't give up. I don't want you to suffer any longer. It's OK to let go. I'll stay here so you won't be alone."

I dry off Mom's upper body and place a fresh blanket across her chest and hips.

"I remember you driving my Mustang to work on the freeway," I say. "Do you remember that?" My fingers tremble as slide off my mother's diaper under the blanket. Closing my eyes, I lift the blanket and sponge down my mother from her waist to her toes, then towel her dry.

"You really love to drive. It's that freedom of the open road. It makes you feel alive."

I smile at the picture of my mom, the steering wheel tight in her grip, careening around the sharp turns of the Pasadena freeway.

I place the blanket back on top of her.

"That's why I couldn't kill myself," I say. "You reminded me how precious life is. You saved me."

My mother's eyes open for a second, and she whispers, "I did?"

I kiss her on the cheek. "Yes, you did."

I roll her over and finish bathing her. I slide a fresh diaper on her waist and wrap her back up in her cocoon.

"You're the best mom anyone could ever have," I say.

With that, my eyes unleash a waterfall of tears. For the first time in many years, I am not embarrassed by my raw emotions. I look at the nightstand. The threadbare book on the nightstand is a bible. I pick it up and place it gently in my mother's left hand, clasping her right in my own. At that moment, my mom squeezes my hand briefly.

"Thank you," I say, "for letting me bathe you."

My mother passed away that night.

Part Five

"What road do I take?" Alice asked.
"Where do you want to go?" the Cheshire Cat said.
"I don't know," Alice answered.
"Then," said the Cat, "it really doesn't matter."[8]

CHAPTER 53

After the funeral, Christy, Joe and I cleared out Mom's house, starting with the attic. I could smell the cobwebs that dangled like broken strings on a violin from the wood rafters. Pine crates climbed to the ceiling like skyscrapers over the dilapidated lower boroughs that were full of dusty furniture, precarious stacks of old china, leather-bound books and cardboard boxes that hadn't seen the light of day since the invention of the hula hoop. As I unpeeled the tape on cardboard lids, memories popped out like a jack in the box. Joe uncovered a box containing all his team photographs from fifteen years of baseball, from T ball to college.

"We're going to need a dumpster," Joe says.

"We'll be moving out of our own house soon," Christy says.

"Too bad there's no equity left in this house," I say. "We might have saved our home."

"Look at this," Joe says. He hands me a stack of handwritten envelopes; inside I discover letters Daniel wrote Mom during his first stay in a sanatorium.

Christy holds up a bright green tubular Christmas ornament. "What's this?"

"The Christmas pickle!" Joe and I shout in unison.

"Never heard of it," Christy says.

"She led a deprived childhood," I say to Joe.

"That explains a lot," he says.

"We'd form a circle around the tree; then Mom would blindfold us," I say. "She'd hang the Christmas pickle and make us fondle the tree blindfolded till someone found it."

"What's the point?" Christy asks.

"Whoever found it got an extra present from Santa and a year of good luck," Joe says.

I pull out a pink pig, with a slot for coins down the middle of his back. The porcelain is cracked.

"We're going broke," I say to Christy.

"We're not any different, just because we're poor."

I turn the empty, cracked pig over in my hands. "But I'm a failure. I can't pay our bills."

"We're more than the sum of our net worth, Erik." She holds up an oversize glass stein. "What do you want to do with this?" Christy asks

"Santa's beer mug!" Joe says. "That's mine."

"OK, but I get the Christmas pickle," I say.

"You left a mug of beer on the mantle for Santa?" Christy says.

"A cold mug of Schlitz and an onion bagel covered with cream cheese," I say.

"You two had some really weird Christmas traditions."

• • •

My past slips away; childhood remembrances sold at the auction house for pennies on the dollar, but they are alive deep within me. Mom will always be clutching the wheel of my Mustang, even though I sold it long ago. The bank may take our house, the home I designed with paper and pencil and plans of retirement, but it's only sticks of wood.

"I've got to leave for work," Joe says. "Box up this stuff and I'll take a load to Goodwill tomorrow." We hug goodbye. Cash is asleep in the corner.

"What did you mean when you said the clinic was the hardest thing you've ever done?" Christy asks. She hands me a stack of emerald green dishes with a crackle glaze.

"I was terrified of myself. What I'd done to you," I say. I wrap a plate in some old newsprint and box it.

"Do you still feel like that?"

"Sometimes, when I wake up in the middle of the night." The paper is dated June 11, 1963. The headline proclaims "Congress passes equal pay act for women."

"Why?"

"I'm afraid I won't be able to fall back to sleep. That's what drove me crazy." I grab another newspaper.

"But you have sleeping pills." Christy wipes the dust off a serving bowl with a rag.

"They don't always work." On the cover is a picture of Neil Armstrong and Buzz Aldrin standing on the moon on July 21, 1969.

Christy stops and turns to me. "I'm afraid you'll lose control of your senses."

"I don't trust myself either." I have to say it. "That's why we can't live together."

The bowl crashes to the floor.

"Are you asking for a divorce?" she asks.

"God no. It would crush me." I place my hand on her shoulder. "You're the reason I'm alive. You stepped between me and the cops."

She puts her arms around my neck and there we stand, over the broken bowl.

"Why did you dare those policemen to shoot you?" she asks.

"I was terrified of going back to the clinic."

"But they were helping you."

"It was something that happened to Daniel."

"What?"

"It was a long time ago."

I kneel down to pick up the shards.

"Talk to me, Erik." I pause for a minute, staring at the floor.

"He caught his roommate stealing a Saint Christopher's metal Mom gave him. It meant the world to him. He got in a brawl and was tied up in a straightjacket in a padded room on tranquilizers for two months. He never was the same after that."

She puts her hand on my head and draws me in to her chest, my knees still pressed to the planks of the floor in front of her. "I'm worried I'll go crazy."

She rubs the scar on her cheek. "Where does that leave me?"

"It means we'll figure it out, together."

Christy is silent. I place the pieces of the bowl in a box, then grab both her hands. "Do you want to dance?" I stand up. "I'm an excellent dancer."

"You have two left feet."

I break into my best moonwalk, a spastic Red-capped Manakin bird in a courting display.[9] My feet slide back and forth across the attic floor while my chunky butt wiggles in reverse across the room. Cash starts to bark.

I shift from the moonwalk to my thriller dance. Cash crouches on all fours and barks even louder, jumping from one side of me to the other.

"Quiet, Cash, you'll disturb the neighbors," Christy says, pressing her index finger against her lips.

I clap my hands over my head, bring them down slowly and drag my feet to one side. Shrugging my shoulders, I turn my head and repeat the step going the other way.

Christy stands like a statue, except for her mouth. It's definitely a smirk.

I break into my zombie crazy shimmy for a good eight seconds then show her my claw hands move, shaking my arms in front of my chest while in a disco pose. Michael Jackson would be impressed.

"You're crazy," she says, smiling.

"I've got papers to prove it."

CHAPTER 54

By the time I return to Tahoe two weeks later, aspen leaves and pine needles are sprinkled across the forest floor. In a cruel twist of fate, a mile from where Cash and I live in our trailer, my dream house sits, taunting.

Foreclosed. Bank owned property. Stay out.

I took the money the bank gave us to vacate our house within thirty days and moved into a trailer that sits on an empty lot one block from Christy's place.

Cash and I walk in the woods. My house has been leveled, uprooted from its foundation, scattered in the wind, sturdy beams, toothpicks on my path. Cash bounds past a mound of chiseled granite, the handsome hearthstone of our fireplace. Deep in my stupor, I trip over the ridge beam of my living room, disguised as a log. A meddlesome grey squirrel chatters at my clumsy feet. Cash chases after it, defending my wounded pride, into the branches of an aging sugar pine, limbs drooping. In front of me a broken bough has fallen across the path, I break off a limb to clear my way and toss it into the woods. Cash chases after it and returns to offer me one end. I grab it. He pulls. I pull back. He digs in his paws and drags me through the woods until I fall, sprawling on the ground but wearing a smile.

He drops the stick in my lap to lick my face.

"I can't believe I lost my house," I say.

"It's not lost," Cash says. "It's right where you left it."

I lie on a patch of pine needles. Cash sits next to me. "I thought I was over talking to you," I say.

"We have more work to do."

"This is going to take longer than I thought."

"We're not making top ramen," Cash says.

"I don't want to be crazy."

"I didn't ask to be born as a dog."

"Help me up," I say.

He bites down on the opposite end of the stick and pulls me upright. He's strong as an ox.

"I didn't lose my house." I say. "The bank took it back."

"So, it was really the bank's house." Cash and I walk, side by side, back towards our trailer.

"It was my dream house."

"That's your ego. You don't need it to be happy."

"But I liked that dream."

"Pick one without a big mortgage, next time."

• • •

When we get back to the trailer Joe is cooking oatmeal and mixing a fruit and kefir smoothie in the blender.

"I've only got a week to get you back on track before I go back to work," he says.

"I don't know where to start."

"We need to clear your head and get focused."

"Remember when I our stole the neighbor's plastic car cover and made a slip and slide with it," I said.

"Mom made us mow his lawn the whole summer."

"She said I was brain dead. That's how I feel lately."

Joe grabs me by the head and shakes my noggin back and forth.

"OK," I say. "Where do we start?"

"First, I've laid out all your medication by the sink, along with a check list for you to mark every time you take a pill. No monkey business, OK?"

"I've learned my lesson."

"Second, let's fill in this calendar with your program for the next three months."

"What program?"

"Altruism is the first part. I have you and Cash doing volunteer work at the hospital."

"You hear that Cash, we're volunteering at the hospital."

Cash perks up his ears.

"Willpower is second. I have you enrolled in a meditation class at For Goodness Sake, a spiritual center in Truckee," Joe says.

"What does that have to do with willpower?"

"Meditation improves self-awareness, focus and self-regulation. That's willpower."

I could use some willpower.

"OK, what's next?" I ask.

"Attitude adjustment. Yours needs a major overhaul."

I knew that one was coming.

"I've called Carson's office to set up a counseling session twice a month. His secretary will call us back later today."

"Knowledge is the fourth part of the program. I ordered some books for you."

"What books?"

"Books by the Dalai Lama, Pema Chodron, Stephen Covey, James Clear, Rick Hanson and Kelly McGonical. Those are the ones to read first."

"There's more?"

"*The Noonday Demon* by Andrew Solomon and *An Unquiet Mind* by Kay R. Jamison, *Darkness Visible* by William Styron and *Sirens* by Joshua Mohr.

Those ones sound scary.

"Exercise is next. You're signed up for a swim program and two weekly appointments with a physical therapist for your back and knee."

"Nutrition is the last part of the program. You're off junk food, permanently. Here's what you'll eat from now on." Joe hands me several sheets of paper with three daily meals planned out for two weeks, each ingredient carefully listed and weighed out.

Hostess Ding Dongs didn't make the cut.

Next, he hands me a calendar.

"What do you think?" he says.

The calendar is peppered with notes written with a red magic marker.

It's bloody frightening.

"You said you were willing to do whatever it takes to get healthy and win Christy back, remember?" Joe says.

CHAPTER 55

The receptionist waves when we enter the hospital annex. "Cash looks handsome today."

"Women love uniforms," Cash says to me.

"Good morning, Gloria," I say.

We walk towards the lounge where a dozen patients from ten years of age to ninety are scattered around the room.

"What's the little blonde girl's name again?" I ask Cash.

"I told you to write it down last week when we met her."

"Come on. You know I'm terrible with names."

Cash nonchalantly scratches his ear with his paw.

"I'll buy you a slider at Burger Me tonight," I say.

"How about a bison burger with grilled onions, pepper jack cheese, avocado and bacon?"

This is extortion.

"Deal."

"The little blonde girl's name is Lisa," Cash says. "She's got leukemia. She's in third grade, loves gymnastics, and is very ticklish.

"Thanks."

I spend the next hour playing second fiddle to Cash as he works his way around the ward. He greets everyone with a windmill tail and a head wag, licks the faces of children till they giggle, rubs his nose into reluctant hands, curls up in bed with complete strangers to ease their pain and sits patiently while an elderly woman in a wheelchair pets him as she and I share memories of her deceased husband. It took six months for Cash to pass the therapy dog certification program, but he was a natural. He connects with people better than I do.

"OK, Cash, say goodbye to Mrs. Williams. I have to drop you off at Christy's."

"Will we see you next week?" she asks.

"You can depend on us, right, Cash?"

He nods. I turn and wave as we walk out the ward.

"You know Cash, volunteering at the hospital really makes me feel good about myself."

"It's all about being there."

"What do you mean?"

"Being in the moment. It's what dog's do."

"Explain."

"We listen to people, not what they say, but how they say it."

"Like body language and tone of voice."

"We absorb what they're feeling and share it."

"That's why I feel so good when I leave the hospital. My sore back and financial problems disappear when I tickle Lisa and watch her giggle."

"You can't feel sorry for yourself when you're helping someone else," Cash says.

"You've gotten pretty good at this wisdom stuff," I say.

"And I'm a chick magnet." Cash says.

CHAPTER 56

It's snowing lightly when Cash and I pull into Christy's driveway. I take a moment to brush the snow off her windshield and set a gift card to her favorite coffee bar on the driver's seat. "Remember what I told you," Cash says.

"Stay calm and smile," I say.

"You're late!" Christy says before I reach the door. She glares at me. I place Cash's mohair blanket, electric toothbrush, chew toys and winter booties on the dining room table. "You conveniently forgot to drop Cash off last Saturday, which was my Saturday night, and now this."

"Sorry. Cash and I were famished. We stopped off for a bite to eat." Cash belches.

"What have you been feeding him?"

"It was just a bite of my burger."

"You're spoiling that dog."

"But he's my best buddy," I say, rubbing his head.

"Erik, we talked about this." She waves her finger in my face. "The vet said Cash needs to lose 10 lbs."

"It was an organic grass-fed bison burger," I say, smiling sheepishly.

"Don't you smirk at me!" she shouts. She turns and stomps out of the room.

"This is your fault!" I say to Cash. He covers his head with his paws.

Christy returns. She's still seething.

"I'm sorry, I don't want to fight like this," I say.

"You don't listen to me," Christy says. Cash begins to chew on the corner of the throw rug.

"Stop that Cash!" she says. Cash creeps out of the room.

"Stay calm," I whisper to myself.

"Are you and Cash talking again?" Christy says.

"**No**, no." I say, stepping back.

Don't lie to her.

She stares at me.

"Not now, sometimes," I say, "but Dr. Williams thinks my new medication will fix that."

She's silent.

"Don't you ever share things with Cash?" I ask.

She wraps her arms around her chest. "You think more of Cash than me."

I shake my head. "That's not true."

"I picked him out," Christy says. "You weren't even there."

"I want the three of us to be a family again."

"He's my dog too."

"I'll feed him whatever you want," I say, I lean in and rub her shoulders.

Her face softens. "And drop him off on time?" she says.

"Like clockwork."

CHAPTER 57

I've landed work as the project architect of a house for an aging hippie who made millions on organic tea balm. It's my first decent job since I left the clinic. It's been a challenging eighteen months.

"Paul, I don't think we can fit a ten-person hot tub inside your master bedroom suite this late in the construction schedule. Robert's crew is about to install the reclaimed oak flooring. Maybe we could incorporate it into the sweat lodge in the back yard. Sure, I can design the tub so your grandkids can cannonball in from the tree house. I'll work on that and send you a sketch in a couple of days. Don't worry, Paul, Robert and I will get it done for you. OK, Namaste to you, too."

"This guy has me running in circles," I say as I set down the phone. Cash sits at my feet.

"You complain because you have no work; you complain when you do," he says.

He's right. I should be more grateful.

"You're more productive when you have a challenge," Cash says.

I do feel creative again. I open up the refrigerator to find a bunch of celery sticks and a tofu sausage.

"I would kill right now for a Snickers bar."

"The intelligent want self-control; children want candy." Cash says, shaking his head.

I've got to stop reading Rumi to my dog.

"I don't understand people's preoccupation with fancy houses and money," Cash says.

"It's how we gauge our success in life."

"I'd better start charging for my advice, then."

"That's shallow," I say.

I'm almost done with the hot tub drawing when I hear a knock on the tin door.

"Hi Paul," I say. He looks like Willie Nelson, with his long grey ponytail and red bandana. "What a surprise." I'm embarrassed as I lead him into my humble trailer.

"I wanted to give this to you in person," he says, handing me an envelope.

"You and Robert have been working your tails off. You're building a house for my kids and grandkids to enjoy, long after I'm gone. It's my dream home, and I want both of you to know how much I appreciate it."

I open the envelope. It's a ticket for two to fly anywhere in the world and a $10,000 check.

"I'm stunned. Thanks," I say.

"The only condition is that you have to finish up the house next month before you take a well-deserved vacation," he says. "Gotta run, I'm taking my granddaughter and her whole class to Disneyland."

CHAPTER 58

"Wake up," Christy yells, rattling the door to my trailer. "We've got class in twenty minutes."

I stumble out of bed and slip into my old work sweats. I rush out the door dripping coffee on the way.

"You won't believe what happened." I say as we walk in the studio.

"Is it good or bad?" she asks.

I watch a dozen energetic women of different shapes and sizes slip off their color coordinated jackets and sweats exposing their bright yoga leggings.

"Want to go on an all expense paid trip to Africa?"

"We're broke, honey. Quit dreaming," Christy says.

I look down at the dried paint spattered on my pants. Suddenly I feel criminally underdressed.

"You'll need these foam blocks for the warrior, archer and lunge poses and don't even try the scorpion, firefly, or locust poses," Christy says.

I'm going into battle with a bunch of insects. How hard could that be?

A petite blonde with a toy poodle tucked under her arm drops her yoga mat on the floor at the head of the class.

"Sherri, you brought Thor today," one of the women sitting in the front row says.

He looks like a mouse with a perm.

"He promised to behave today, didn't you?" Sherri says, holding the rug rat inches from her nose. Thor licks her face.

A chorus of "He's sooo cute," reverberates from the front row.

"Ignoring the fact we're broke," I ask, "would you go with me?"

"Maybe, but why Africa?" Christy says.

"It's something Carson and I have talked about, facing my fears."

Sherri sets Thor on the floor, lights a few sticks of incense in a bowl and turns on some soft foreign music. It's Bom Diggy Diggy.

I have a sudden craving for some dal bhaji and a chapatti.

"OK, Class. I want you to all stand up and reach your hands to the sky."

"Now bend forward and touch your toes," the instructor says.

"Just reach for your shins," Christy whispers.

I hear my back creak but I'm oblivious. I'm transfixed by all the graceful female limbs moving around me.

"Will it be dangerous?" Christy asks.

"No more so than yoga, I say."

Over the next half hour, I'm vaguely aware of the downward dog and dolphin plank and cat and cow and I sweat and strain and grunt like a pig and try to mimic the movements of the supple bodies around me that bend and stretch and balance like the snowflake ballerinas in the Nutcracker suite. Thor walks down the line getting coos and being petted. He scrutinizes the form of each yoga pose we strike like a marine corps drill instructor inspecting the recruits in boot camp. I try to keep up, but my back spasms and I collapse in a heap on my sweat drenched yoga mat and

Thor looks at me with an air of utter contempt just as I let loose a butt yodel.

All eyes turn and I clutch my back. “Bad dog!” I say, crawling out of the room, humbled and exhausted with Christy close behind me.

“Are you OK?” she asks.”

I have a whole new respect for the petite blonde yoga instructor and all those female athletes, especially Christy.

“I just pulled a muscle.”

CHAPTER 59

The bright red sash and intricate black braids of the customs officer are striking, as is her smile. "Welcome to Rwanda," she says.

A broad-shouldered man holding a hand-written sign, *Mr. and Mrs. Scott,* greets us outside the glass doors in the sweltering heat.

"Hello, my name is John," he says, shaking our hands. He carries both our suitcases to a sparling green Toyota Landcruiser. "Welcome, come, come… follow me."

"I left the engine running and the AC on for you," he says.

"Thank you," I say, "I'm Erik and this is my wife Christy."

"Is it always this hot?" Christy says.

"We're having a heat wave, 86 degrees today, our hottest day of the year." He places our bags in the back and jumps in the driver's seat, quickly closing the door. "Chilled water," he says. He places a steel water bottle in our hands.

For three hours, John points out local landmarks and weaves stories from tribal Rwanda to Belgium colonization through national independence in 1962. Christy and I hold hands in the backseat and watch clusters of thatch roofed huts fly past on the verdant hillsides. We stop on a ridge to take pictures; a young mother steps out of roadside stand with a baby slung across her hip. Six children, peek out from behind their mother. Shyly, they smile and wave.

"May I take your picture?" Christy asks.

"La Madame veut prendre ta photo," John says.

The mother nods and then lines up her children, the ascending steps of her family, from youngest to oldest, in front of a rusted Coca Cola sign that decorates the earthen shelter. I make faces and stick out my tongue between clicks of Christy's camera; giggles erupt, breaking the children from their wooden poses. The children are thin as rails. I pull out some money to offer the mother, but John shakes his head.

"Is it OK if we buy some snacks?" I ask. He nods. We walk out with enough bananas and cookies to feed a small army and drive off to a children's chorus of *bye bye*.

"Where did you learn French?" I ask.

"I started French in third grade."

"What did you speak before that?" I ask.

"Kinyarwanda and Kiswahili," John says.

"If you don't mind my asking, why do you drive tourists around in a Landcruiser?" Christy says.

"It's the same reason Willie Sutton robbed banks," he says with a good-natured laugh. "That's where the money is."

"Have you always been a driver?" I ask.

"No. I inherited a small plot of land from my father. I still farm it, but I became a teacher."

On a barren hillside a large white cross with "**Never Again**" written across the arms of the cross comes into view. I'm startled. The sight strikes a chord deep within me.

"What's that?" I ask.

"That's a memorial to the genocide victims," John says.

I lost my sanity too, though it was nothing compared to the genocide here. "I read about it, but I never understood," I say.

"The reasons are both intricately complex and quite simple," John says.

"Give us the simple one," I say.

I lost hope.

"Colonial powers gave us ethnic ID cards and then turned the Tutsis against the Hutus. For hundreds of years, a Tutsi was a wealthy noble and a Hutu was a farmer. It had little to do with race. We learned to hate one another."

I hated myself.

"I'm surprised to see a memorial out here in the countryside," I say.

"We have them in almost every town," John says. "We don't want to forget what happened, so we commemorate it every April 7th."

April is the month I went into the clinic.

"Many countries would just want to put it behind them," I say.

I certainly do.

We pass another sign. It reads, **Kwigirira Ikezere** and **Kwinhangana.**

"What does that mean?" I ask.

"The first one means strong heart," John says. "The second is trust in the future and others. We need to find hope and meaning out of trauma."

CHAPTER 60

A white ring of cloud surrounds the jungle flanks of Mount Karisimba's pyramid peak as we approach park headquarters. Almost every square inch of arable land is under cultivation, right up to the ascending mountain sides. "That's the biggest threat to the mountain gorillas," John says. "We're destroying the last of their habitat by burning the jungle to grow more crops. My farm is right along the base of the mountain. I grow potatoes alongside the jungle."

"Do the gorillas ever leave the jungle?" Christy asks.

"Only when they want to steal my potatoes," he says, "so I make up my losses by driving tourists to see them."

John introduces us to a park ranger, Rugira, as we unload our daypacks and camera. We're joined by a German and Canadian couple who look to be as excited as we are.

"Be aware of the nettles as we climb through the jungle today," Rugira says. "We've been assigned the *Amahoro* gorilla group, which means "peaceful." Ubumwe, the dominant silverback, is very easy going and calm."

I never imagined a gorilla to be easy going.

"But Ubumwe is being challenged by Charles, the second silverback in this group, for dominance. They've been fighting continuously for a week," Rugira says.

"Is it safe to be around them?" Christy asks. She wonders the same thing about me.

"Charles and Ubumwe are focused on their own battle. They won't bother us," Rugira says. "If either of them approaches, stand still and don't look them directly in the eyes. Cast your gaze downward. It's a sign of submission."

My mouth is suddenly caked with chalk and my knees feel weak. I didn't sign up to take on a 500-pound gorilla.

There's a crackle on the two-way radio strapped to Rugira's hip. He converses with someone in what I assume is Kinyarwanda.

"The trackers have located the gorillas. It will take three hours to reach them, but the trail is flat, till the last mile."

Rugira helps us crawl over a volcanic stone wall that separates the open farmland from the dense jungle. The morning sun disappears behind the lush canopy as we step over downed trees, covered with clumps of moss. After two hours of tromping through thick mud and damp vegetation, we stop at a clearing and catch a glimpse of blue sky.

"If this is a trail," the Canadian man says, "I'll hate to see what bushwhacking through the jungle is like."

Rugira checks with the trackers on his radio again, while we wipe beads of sweat off our brows and drink copious volumes of water.

"We're close," Rugira says. "They're just over that ridge." He points to a knoll straight up the hillside.

Single file, we climb. No one talks. We draw in as much air as our lungs will allow. The tall trees give way to thickets of vines with prickly leaves as wide as dinner plates. We wind our way past ferns that sprout dozens of fronds and short stands of bamboo. With the sky exposed, the sun beats down on my shaved head and the muddy trail turns firm; the dried mud falls off my boots. I grab a limb to pull myself up. I hope my knee holds out.

Two muscular men in green fatigues greet us near the top. The younger one has a rifle slung over his shoulder. The other holds a machete. They look threatening, except for their broad smiles.

"You've made it," they say. One pats me on the back and the other helps Christy up the last steep pitch.

"We'll stay in a group," Rugira says, "and keep at least ten feet from the gorillas at all times."

Christy grabs my hand. "Are you OK?" Christy asks. I ignore the butterflies in my stomach and nod.

Rugira points to a clearing up ahead. A baby gorilla holds tight to the back of its mother as she walks across our trail on her knuckled hands. She turns her head but barely acknowledges us, continuing her stroll towards four other females picking bamboo leaves. A half dozen other youngsters wrestle and chase one another in an open expanse of low vegetation. We follow the trackers to the edge of the clearing.

A deep rumbling sound emanates from the bushes across from the foraging females. A huge male with silver hair down his back steps out into the open. He looks battered; there's a gash across his forehead and his right hand is bloodied. He stands up and beats his chest, letting out a grunt.

Rugira gathers us together. "That's Charles," he says. "He's posturing for Ubumwe." A second, even larger silverback rambles across the clearing towards Charles. Ubumwe has his teeth bared and raises his massive arms. The two gorillas collide, pummeling one another with quick blows; then they back off, while the females shriek in the background. Ubumwe walks around Charles, who turns to keep his eye on his adversary. Stunned by the display of brute force, I'm frozen in place. I should be terrified, but I'm more fascinated than frightened.

"Take some pictures," Christy says. I raise my camera as the two size one another up. Neither backs down. I hear cameras click all around me. I struggle to focus the lens on my camera as we huddle in a small circle only forty feet away. I notice the females and younger gorillas do the same. They are tightly bunched and holding one another.

Charles lunges at Ubumwe, who pushes Charles away. They circle like two heavyweight wrestlers, slapping at one another in quick exchanges; but no real damage is inflicted. The fight continues for several minutes. They look exhausted. Finally, they sit down just a few feet apart.

"What's going on?" Christy asks.

"They're resting between rounds," a tracker says. "They've been doing this for several days, without sleep. They won't let down their guard."

"No, this is something else," Rugira says. "The two of them are back to back. Listen: no loud grunts. They're making softer sounds."

"Are they talking?" I ask.

"We recognize twenty-six distinct vocalizations the gorillas use to communicate, but I'm sure they have more," Rugira says.

The two gorillas lean against one another. I'd love to understand what they're saying.

After several minutes, Charles gets up and walks over to the group of females and youngsters. They cower, their bellies on the ground and hands hidden from view. Ubumwe watches dispassionately. Charles picks out a few females and they follow him off into the bush with their offspring.

The remaining females walk back to Ubumwe. The eldest one carefully grooms him as the youngsters surround them.

"What just happened?" I ask.

"Rather than fight to the death, Ubumwe allowed Charles to take several females to start his own group."

I bet Ubumwe could have beaten Charles. He was stronger. Killing his brother wasn't worth it.

The tension fades and the youngsters begin playing again. The youngest one approaches us, his curiosity piqued by all the clicking cameras. When he gets ten feet away, Ubumwe lets out a loud grunt. The little guy turns and runs straight into his mother's arms.

"Dad just warned the little one to keep his distance from us," Rugira says.

Two other youngsters approach Ubumwe and poke him in the chest. He grabs them and playfully rolls them onto his stomach. They jump up and down on his massive chest. He seems to be enjoying himself.

"I thought the females raise the children," the German woman says.

"That's usually the case, but Ubumwe likes to play with the little ones," Rugira says.

Ubumwe is comfortable in his own skin. Rather than violence, he chose family. I want to do the same.

I control who I am. I don't need to be afraid of myself any longer.

CHAPTER 61

Fields of white pyrethrum flowers carpet the farmland as Christy and I walk back along the edges of a red dirt road towards our lodge. The flowers sway with the wind, their stalks raising and falling like fans at a baseball game doing the wave across the length of the bleachers.

"What did you think of the gorillas?" I ask.

"They were frightening at first. The males were violent but they settled their differences and by the end I thought they were magnificent." Christy tucks her arm under my shoulder as we approach our bungalow on the cobbled path.

"I had no idea they would be so humanlike," I say.

"You seemed to be in a trance watching the silverback."

"Ubumwe was fascinating," I say. "He made me realize I can choose how I'm going to be." We kick off our muddy boots on the porch.

"What do you mean?"

I unlock the bamboo door. The bloom of flowers on the nightstand fills the room with the fragrance of bougainvillea.

"I'm free to be myself with you. I'm not afraid. The gorilla in my head was only my self-destructive fears."

"Do you ever hear my thoughts?" She starts to unbutton her blouse.

"Sort of, the gorilla screams in my ears, yours is more of a whisper."

"What does my voice say to you?" She unbuttons her travel shirt and lets it slide to the floor.

"It tells me you love me." I pull my shirt over my head.

"You should listen to that whisper." She reaches behind her and unclips her bra.

"It also tells me to turn on the dishwasher when it's full of dirty dishes," I say.

She laughs. "That baby gorilla was so adorable." She unzips her cargo pants and steps out of them.

"Not as adorable as you look to me right now," I say.

"It's nice to see your abs again," Christy says, poking me in the stomach. She slips out of her panties and tosses them onto my bare shoulder.

"Are you joining me?" she asks, turning on the shower.

"Would you have married me," I ask. "knowing I was going to go bankrupt at fifty-seven?" My boxers fall to the floor.

"I didn't marry you for your money. You were penniless when we met, remember?"

I stand, completely naked, and quiver inside. "Would you have married me knowing I was going to go crazy?"

"I married you with my eyes wide open, knowing your family had a history of mental illness." She grabs my hand and pulls me into the shower.

Bubbles swirl at our feet as we lather each other with coconut shampoo. The sensation of cool water, slippery suds and her skin sliding across mine is delicious. We enjoy the remainder of the afternoon making love.

I wake up from my mid-day slumber with Christy's head on my arm.

PART SIX

"It's no use going back to yesterday,
because I was a different person then."[10]

CHAPTER 62

It's been two years since Mom died. Christy and I renewed our marriage vows on the beach at Lake Tahoe. Joe was our minister. Christy, Cash and I are planning a road trip to the Grand Canyon and hunting on Craigslist for a trailer. I designed a tiny house for the three of us. Cash and I still talk, though he's getting to be a better listener. He's explains the meaning of life to me and I'm teaching him how to squat over a toilet. He's pretty smart for a dog. Other than Cash, I haven't had any hallucinations in two years. Dr. Williams says I may have to live with that. I meditate twenty minutes a day and contemplate my navel. I can't determine if it's an "inny" or an "outy", but I'm OK with that. I have years to resolve my dilemma. Carson offers a free therapy class for all his former patients from the clinic once a year. I decide to drive down for a visit. I love freebies.

Walking through the front door of the clinic, a flood of emotion washes over me. I take a seat on the tired couch in the entry to catch my breath, surprised my wounds are still tender. No one notices my scar, yet the memory of my anguish in this building throbs beneath my skin. Charles stands in the hallway. He breaks into a smile when he sees me, exposing a mouthful of freshly bleached teeth as he walks over. His new goatee looks more grey than black but his handshake is strong. His long sturdy fingers swallow my hand in his.

"How are you, Charles?"

"Good. I work in a grocery store and teach Lakota."

"How are you and Christy doing?" he asks.

"Good. I think we're closer after all we've been through together."

"You seem much more at ease."

"I'm learning to trust myself, even when I have an occasional night of insomnia."

"In Lakota culture, to find closeness with the Great Spirit sometimes a message comes through nature in the form of an animal or bird. We call it a spirit guide."

"That's interesting," I say. If only Charles knew. "How's your twelve-step program?"

"I take it one day at a time," he says. "You'd better head in, the seats are filling up."

When I enter, I see Gina unstacking chairs in the front of the room. "This looks like the bar scene from Star Wars," I say.

Gina turns and breaks into a smile. "I guess I'm never going to live that down," she says as we embrace.

"How are you and Noah?"

"He's growing like a weed. I'm a security guard at an elementary school."

"That sounds like the perfect job."

"Can you put these two chairs along the front row?"

"Sure thing." I catch a glimpse of Sandy sitting in the front row. Her blonde hair falls in waves down her face. I set down the chairs next to her.

"I didn't recognize you without your pajamas," I say. I bend over to give her a hug.

"I burned those the day I left the clinic."

"How are you?" I ask.

"OK. I see Carson once a week and tutor Gina's son, Noah, two nights."

"You must be part of Gina's pole dancing class."

"I'm not **that** cured!"

As we talk, Carson enters the room, pushing an atrophied man with a shaved head in a wheelchair. It's Alex.

Sandy, Gina and I rush over. "You're alive!" I say.

"Barely," he says. "The cancer went into remission for a year then came back six months ago with a vengeance."

"Are you on chemo?" Gina asks.

"I stopped all treatment a month ago," Alex says, holding back tears. "It's spread everywhere."

"Let's settle down everyone," Carson calls out.

Sandy wheels Alex over to the front row and I take a seat in the back. It's painful to see Alex in such a state.

"Thanks for coming. I want each of you to write down the most important lesson you learned at the clinic and your biggest challenge, now you're out. I'll give you a few minutes and then we'll share."

For the next hour, patients tell their tales of recovery and relapse, self-hatred and self-discovery, emotional trauma and healing. Everyone tries to exorcise their private demons as best they can. Some fend off the terror that strangles them in their sheets through the power of prayer or wailing and tears, while others listen to the music of Bach and chant mantras. Some fight back with fists of rage; others bare knuckle the ride. Each person finds what works for them. As the evening comes to a close, Carson asks Charles to come to the front of the room. Gina walks over to Charles and hands him a partial roll of toilet paper wrapped in a blue ribbon. Charles looks down, lifting his glasses onto his bald head. "You're giving me a roll of T.P. for the road?"

"Open it," Gina says. Charles unties the ribbon and the paper unfurls down to the floor, revealing some beautifully written text that descends down the paper.

Charles lowers his eyeglasses. "In recognition of your many hours of study, and multiyear commitment to our program," he stops to unravel the roll, "the Combine County Behavioral Health Sciences Clinic, hereby bestows on Charles Eagle Brown the honorary title of master of pharmacological substance abuse, specializing in Methamphetamine addiction."

"It's your diploma," Gina says. She stands on her toes and plants a kiss on Charles's cheek.

"Thank you, this will look great on my resume," Charles says, carefully rolling the toilet paper back onto the cylinder.

"Where's my diploma?" I ask.

"You're only a sophomore," Gina says.

"Let's have a few minutes of quiet prayer for Alex," Carson says after the laughter subsides. I hear a dozen voices whisper prayers around me. Alex sits in his wheelchair in the front of the room with his eyes closed.

A voice sings a cappella from across the room. The tone is strong and clear.

Amazing Grace, how sweet the sound,
That saved a wretch like me."
I once was lost but now am found,
Was blind, but now I see.

Several people start to sing along. Soon, more voices join in. I stand up and join in the chorus. I'm a better person for knowing Alex, Charles, Gina and Sandy.

Yea, when this flesh and heart shall fail,
And mortal life shall cease,

I shall possess, within the veil.
A life of joy and peace.[11]

When the song ends, the patients converge around Alex like the petals of a poppy that fold inward when the sun sets over the horizon.

• • •

I say my goodbyes and I'm left alone in an empty parking lot. Cash's head pokes out of the cab of my truck.

"Let's surprise Christy and buy some fresh salmon for the barbecue tonight," I say as we drive off."

"Great idea," Cash says.

We take the scenic way home, driving over Spooner summit and down the winding highway that careens past steep cliffs and dense forests of pine and fir. Pine cones and sand litter the narrow shoulder of the asphalt ribbon that unfolds around each curve.

"Part of me is glad I went crazy," I say.

He peers at me with his head cocked. I rub between his ears.

"Christy and Joe showed me I was worth saving, even at my worst."

"They believed in you when you didn't believe in yourself," Cash says, "don't ever forget that." I nod.

"I have something important to tell you," I say.

His ears perk up.

"I won't be talking to you anymore."

He sits up.

"But we're best friends."

"That will never change," I say, rubbing his belly.

"Are you ready to start the next chapter of your life?"

"I am."

"Then my work is done," he says. "Make yourself proud."

"You're my inner thoughts, buddy, the best ones."

He rests his head on my lap as we drive off, meandering along the rocky shoreline of Lake Tahoe. The highway snakes its way past the prehistoric granite outcroppings that sit half submerged in the clear waters like giant dinosaur eggs at Sand Harbor. A cool breeze sweeps through the open cab of the truck, laced with the vanilla scent of Jeffrey pine bark. Above the tree line, an osprey unfurls his feather sails and soars over the panorama of Lake Tahoe. The osprey's wings retract and he dives down to pluck a trout from the pristine water, the rainbow colors of the fish shimmering against soft blue sky.

Cash is part of me, just like Mom and Daniel and my gorilla. Voices that whisper and sometimes scream, fragments of the people floating inside my brain. Words that only I can hear.

THE END

Author's Note

In memory of my uncle, Paul Gilberg, my father, Harry Gilberg, my brother, Richard Gilberg, and my friends, Chris F. and Frank D. I never understood what you went through, till I stood at the edge of the same precipice.

All the profits from this book will be donated to promote mental health advocacy.

ACKNOWLEDGEMENTS

To my wife, Karyn and sister Diane, I will forever cherish your love, bravery and support. I would not be alive, if not for you.

To the band of brothers who reached out and shared their own troubles with me, Peter Newman, Andy Kuhnmuench, Joe Bayliss, David Moore, Gordon Mandeno, and Michael Wurtz. You're a bunch of whackos and I'm proud to include myself in our fraternity.

To Douglas Perry, whose sense of humor and dedication to his aunt, my mother, I will always appreciate.

To the staff of For Goodness Sake, Truckee, Calif., especially Jackie Griffin and Jon L. Weedn. Thanks for introducing me to the mystery of meditation. By my calculations, it will take me ten more reincarnations to reach nirvana. I may need an extension on my library books.

To Reuben Reynolds, RN BHS CM, my health insurance caseworker, thanks for your kindness.

To Karen Terry, without your sensitive encouragement and poetic insights this book would not exist. You were selfless. www.tangledrootswriting.com

To my editor, Joshua Mohr. Your creative inspiration, personal commitment and intimate understanding of the craft of writing made this literary journey of mine incredibly rich. You're a miracle worker. Thanks mate. www.joshuamohr.net

To my Beta readers, Corey Leibow, Kathleen Bell, Bat Goddard, Jill Shalvis, Denise Eyton-Lloyd, Ron Currie, Matt Symmonds, Nancy Irwin and Jody Miller. Your perceptive insights into the reader experience were invaluable. To Corey, in particular, you were a glutton for punishment.

To all the writers who inspired me, especially Paul Harding, Ken Kesey, Jeannette Walls, Christopher Moore, Alexandra Fuller, Franklin Russel, Viet Thanh Nguyen and Bill Watterson.

To Grant Clowers, LCSW, thank you for your wisdom, guidance and patience. You tossed a life preserver to a drowning man.

To Lynne Reilly, MFT, LADC, thanks for your friendship, guidance and understanding. Kirk would be proud of you.

To Steven Holroyd, MD, thanks for your sound counsel and professional expertise with my medication.

To David Chase, who helped me realize Prozac is much more recognized as an antidepressant than Lexapro, hence my final book title, Love and Prozac. I'll be looking for you and your boys on the ski slope in Big Sky, Montana.

To Dr. Gail Pritchard, thank you for convincing me not to get too technical on the details of psychiatric medication in my novel. I'd rather leave that to the experts, such as yourself.

To the entire staff at the Carson Tahoe Behavioral Health Clinic, thank you for your kindness and dedication. Know that you made a difference in my life.

To my fellow patients at the clinic, your compassion for one another, despite your own intense suffering, displayed a generosity of spirit I will always remember.

"One of the deep secrets of life is that all that is really worth the doing is what we do for others."[12]

Lewis Carrol

About the Author

Gary Gilberg is a professional life and executive coach. He volunteers at Project Mana, the Tahoe Safe Alliance and For Goodness Sake in Truckee, California. He can be reached by email at 2coachgary@gmail.com.

End Notes

[1] Lewis Carroll, (1832-1898) Alice's Adventures in Wonderland (1865)

[2] Prozac would not commonly be prescribed under these circumstances. Lexapro would be a better choice, since Erik has insomnia.

[3] Lewis Carroll, (1832-1898) Alice's Adventures in Wonderland (1865)

[4] Lewis Carroll, (1832-1898) Alice's Adventures in Wonderland (1865)

[5] A psychiatrist would typically have a much longer and more detailed discussion with his patient about his hallucinations, what's behind them, treatment options, medication side effects, etc. I chose not to include those details in my novel.

[6] Bill Watterson, The Essential Calvin and Hobbes, page 100, copyright 1988 by Andrew McMeel Publishing, Reprinted with permission.

[7] Lewis Carroll, (1832-1898) Alice's Adventures in Wonderland (1865)

[8] Lewis Carroll, (1832-1898) Alice's Adventures in Wonderland (1865)

[9] Moonwalk Manakin Bird, YouTube, May 30, 2011

[10] Lewis Carroll, (1832-1898) Alice's Adventures in Wonderland (1865)

[11] John Newton, (1725-1807) Amazing Grace (1779)

[12] Lewis Carroll, (1832-1898) The Letters of Lewis Carroll (1885)

Made in the USA
Columbia, SC
03 September 2019